Down *to the* Bonny Glen

The **MARTHA** *Years*
By Melissa Wiley
Illustrated by Renée Graef

LITTLE HOUSE IN THE HIGHLANDS
THE FAR SIDE OF THE LOCH

Down *to the* Bonny Glen

Melissa Wiley

Illustrations by Renée Graef

HarperCollins*Publishers*

For ole Fred

*The author wishes to thank Caroline
Carr-Locke for her invaluable assistance
in researching the customs and culture
of late eighteenth-century Scotland.*

HarperCollins®, 🏠®, Little House®, and The Martha Years™
are trademarks of HarperCollins Publishers Inc.

Down to the Bonny Glen
Text copyright © 2001 by HarperCollins Publishers Inc.
Illustrations copyright © 2001 by Renée Graef
Printed in the United States of America. For information address
HarperCollins Children's Books, a division of HarperCollins Publishers,
1350 Avenue of the Americas, New York, NY 10019.
www.littlehousebooks.com

Library of Congress Cataloging-in-Publication Data
Wiley, Melissa.
    Down to the bonny glen / Melissa Wiley ; illustrations by Renée
Graef.
    p.   cm.
    Summary: In Scotland in 1791, eight-year-old Martha Morse, who
would grow up to become the great-grandmother of author Laura
Ingalls Wilder, meets her new governess and learns the difference
between growing up a laird's daughter and a child of a cottager.
    ISBN 0-06-027985-0 — ISBN 0-06-028204-5 (lib. bdg.)
    ISBN 0-06-440714-4 (pbk.)
    1. Morse, Martha—Juvenile fiction. [1. Morse, Martha—Fiction.
2. Wilder, Laura Ingalls, 1867–1957—Family—Fiction.
3. Governesses—Fiction.   4. Scotland—History—18th century—
Fiction.] I. Graef, Renée, ill.   II. Title.   III. Series.
PZ7.W64634 Do 2001   00-053510
[Fic]—dc21

1   2   3   4   5   6   7   8   9   10
❖
First Edition, 2001

Contents

The Wedding-Day Morn 1

Penny Wedding 16

Copywork 45

Bundling the Flax 56

A Lesson Learned 77

Cat, Mouse, and Hedgehog 91

The Cauldron on the Moor 102

When the Cat's Away 119

Miss Lydia Crow 145

House Tour 157

More Copywork 170

Culloden and the Crofter 186

Dance at Fairlie 201

Next Morning 215

The Men Who Killed the Trees 227

Handsel Monday 235

Grisie's Suitors 260

The Lads Come Home 274

The Cottage Beyond the Wood 292

The Mare's Ride 311

Down *to the* Bonny Glen

The Wedding-Day Morn

On the morning of Nannie's wedding, Martha could not sit still. Nor stand still. She bobbed back and forth between the nursery table and the window so many times during breakfast that Miss Norrie, her governess, turned almost purple with dismay. Martha couldn't help it: the suspense was dreadful. Everyone in the Stone House, except perhaps for the governess, was anxious to see whether the sun would manage to break free from the heavy mantle of clouds that covered the sky.

As soon as Martha had gulped down the last of her porridge, she ran downstairs to the kitchen, leaving Miss Norrie's fluttering protests behind in the nursery. Breathlessly she stationed herself at the garden door to keep watch for any glint of sunlight that might penetrate the clouds. She called out frequent reports to Cook, who stood red-faced and grim at the hearthfire, stirring her beef broth and turning the legs of mutton she had set to roast on a spit.

"'Tis a terrible shame, that's what," Cook muttered, cranking the handle of the spit. Droplets of mutton fat hissed in the dripping-pan below. "If ivver a lass deserved a fine weddin' day, 'tis our Nannie. A kinder, more good-natured lass ye'll no find in all Scotland— nor England besides. And that Gerald's a fine, stouthearted lad. Sure and they dinna deserve such a parcel o' ill luck!"

Her voice was so fierce that Martha came inside to look at her. Cook was glaring at the mutton legs as if they were to blame for the poor weather. Martha understood exactly how she felt. Rain on Nannie's wedding day would be a terrible misfortune. Everyone said so. Cook had gone around for days muttering the old rhyme,

"Happy's the bride the sun shines on;
Happy's the corpse the rain falls on."

At least it was not raining, not yet. But the sun must shine—it *must*, Martha said to herself, and that was all there was to it. Nannie was too dear a person not to deserve a lucky wedding day.

"Why is it bad luck if the sun doesna shine?" Martha asked Cook. "I can see how rain might spoil the wedding day, but I dinna see why it's bad luck on the marriage."

"Whisht, child, I dinna make the rules; I only mind them," Cook scolded.

"But who did make them? Did God make them? I dinna see why He would make a silly rule like that," Martha protested. "It doesna seem fair. 'Tis no fault o' Nannie and Gerald's if it rains on their wedding day. They canna help it one way or the other."

Cook did not answer; she only frowned harder at her kettle of broth.

"Alisdair says all this bother about omens and luck is just superstition," Martha went on. "He says it doesna really mean a thing. He says we ought to remember that it's 1791, practically the nineteenth century, and we mustna cling to the foolish notions of the auld days."

"Ah, yer brother says that, does he?" Cook answered sharply. "I suppose that's the sort o' tomfoolery they teach them at them fancy city schools nowadays. 'Nearly the nineteenth century' indeed. As if the sun and the rain take any heed o' what century it is." She gave a disdainful snort to show what she thought of what she called "high-steppin' book learnin'."

"Och," she added, shaking her head, "when I think o' what yer father's payin' to have that lad's head stuffed full o' nonsense . . ."

"Miss Martha dear!" Miss Norrie's voice

came trilling down from the top of the stairs. "Where did you run off to? You must come and let me dress your hair!"

Martha sighed. Having to have her hair brushed seemed always to happen in the middle of the most interesting conversations. But then Miss Norrie seemed to think hair brushing was necessary some half dozen times a day. Miss Norrie said she had never in her life seen someone whose hair ran as wild as Martha's. "But I suppose it's to be expected," she always added, "when one insists upon dashing about out-of-doors in all weathers without benefit of hat nor bonnet!"

Miss Norrie did not approve of allowing young ladies to spend too much time out-of-doors. Miss Norrie, it seemed to Martha, did not entirely approve of *her*. Martha had wanted very much to like Miss Norrie when she arrived last spring. Martha had never had a governess before. Her cousins, Rachel and Mary, who lived in a house called Fairlie on the other side of Loch Caraid, had a kind and gentle governess whom they liked very much. And their governess, Miss Caldwell, liked them; she was always saying so. Miss Caldwell said eight-year-old Rachel was the best-behaved young lady she had ever had the pleasure to know. She said Mary had nicer manners at age six than some girls twice her age.

During the past six months, Miss Norrie had many things to say upon the subject of Martha's manners, but none of them were comfortable to hear.

Sometimes Martha wished Miss Caldwell could be her governess instead of the cousins'. But then would come the unsettling thought that perhaps Miss Caldwell would have the same opinions about Martha that Miss Norrie did. After all, it could not be denied that Miss Norrie was herself a kind and gentle person. She was gentle and delicate as a flower—a flower trembling in a breeze. Miss Norrie did not seem to require a very strong breeze to be set a-trembling. Small things, like an over-turned inkwell or muddy footprints on the nursery floor—these were enough to set off a great fluttering and hand-wringing in the thin, pale-haired governess.

"Miss Martha!" Miss Norrie called again, and Martha winced. She had not meant to stand woolgathering. Mum had told her many times she must never keep her governess waiting.

She resisted the temptation to run outside for a last look at the sky.

"I must go," she told Cook, who nodded without looking up from the hearth. Martha hurried out of the kitchen—resisting another temptation to stop in the larder and peek at Hedgie, asleep in his box with his fat round body half buried in the straw and his little pointed nose resting on his dear black paws. The hedgehog deserved his sleep, anyhow, after a busy night of hunting the insects that dared to venture into Cook's kitchen.

Martha wheeled around the corner to the hallway, and then, remembering suddenly how it upset Miss Norrie when she ran, she forced herself to walk. The governess was waiting at the top of the steps with the hairbrush in her hand.

"There you are, dear," she murmured. "You weren't disturbing the cook again, were you? You must learn to leave the servants alone, Miss Martha dear, and allow them to get on with their work."

Martha's blood grew hot within her. Miss Norrie was always saying things like that. They were maddening statements—as if Cook weren't dearer to Martha than anyone in the world except her own parents and brothers and sister! "The cook," indeed! And "the servants"—as if they were not people with names. *Nannie* was one of the servants, or at any rate she had been until today. And was not Mum herself planning to wear her yellow silk to Nannie's wedding?

Martha stood halfway up the stairs, staring at Miss Norrie. There were a great many things she wanted to say to the governess, and she knew she must not say any of them. Instead she squeezed her lips tight and walked slowly the rest of the way up the staircase.

"Oh, heavens, such a fright you look," fluttered Miss Norrie. "Miss Martha dear, when *will* you learn not to go downstairs without having made your proper toilet? Suppose a guest came calling?"

"I'd hide in the kitchen," said Martha wickedly, and then she bit her lip, for she had promised Mum she would try not to be impertinent. There were so many promises to remember, now that she was eight and a half years old and expected to behave like a young lady.

Miss Norrie herded Martha to the nursery and made her sit down to have her hair brushed. The brush yanked and pulled its way through the red tangles. Martha missed the days when her sister Grisie had been the one to brush her hair. Grisie was sharper tongued than Miss Norrie, but her hands were more patient. Grisie was nearly seventeen years old now, almost grown up. She had a great many things to do with her time. She could no longer be expected to look after a little sister—after all, that was what a governess was for.

Last spring, just before Miss Norrie came, Father had hired men to divide the large upstairs nursery into two smaller rooms. One became a bedchamber for Grisie. She had a new four-poster bed hung with flowing blue curtains, and a rosewood writing table with a matching chair. Grisie had embroided the cushion for the chair herself. She had sewn tiny pink rosebuds all around the edge of the bedcurtains, too, so that the bed was like a summer sky above a rose garden. It was a lovely room. Martha hated it with all her might.

The other room had become the new nursery. It was small and plain, crowded with furniture. Martha shared the nursery with Miss Norrie now. Miss Norrie had taken Grisie's place in the old box bed, and the bed Duncan and Robbie used to sleep in was shoved in the far corner next to the clothespress. Alisdair's old bed had been moved up into the attic. When Martha's brothers came home from school for their short holidays, she and Miss Norrie moved into the guest bed downstairs in the parlor so that the boys could have the nursery. Miss Norrie did not think it proper to sleep in the same room as the boys. But the boys were never home for long. It seemed to Martha as though a year had passed since their last visit, though it had only been a month. She missed Duncan, especially.

"Ouch!" she cried, for Miss Norrie's brush had encountered a particularly fearsome snarl.

"Hold still, dear, and it won't hurt you so," the governess soothed.

Martha did not think she had been moving.

She tried to set her mind on something besides hair. Perhaps Mum would allow her to go to Nannie's mother's house before the wedding. Some of the guests had probably gathered there already, crowding into the little thatched hut, eating curds and cream with the spoons they had brought from their own homes. Soon the groomsmen would come to fetch Nannie. . . .

The more Martha thought about it, the more she ached to go. She stood as still as she possibly could and did not make a single sound during the rest of the yanking and pulling. At last the red curls were reasonably tamed, and Miss Norrie was satisfied that the ribbon which kept the hair out of Martha's eyes was tied in a perfect bow. Miss Norrie always spent a long time over the bow, for it was important to her that the ends come out even.

Martha ran to the clothespress to take out her pink dress. Mollie, the housemaid, had washed and ironed it for the wedding. Miss Norrie wrung her hands and said she feared to see what state that lovely frock would be in by the day's end, but she helped Martha into it nonetheless. Mum had said Martha must wear her best frock, for the cousins would be wearing theirs. But the cousins were only going to the kirk for the ceremony; they would not join the wedding party for the festivities afterward. That would not be proper, for Nannie was not their servant. Martha felt sorry for them; Rachel and Mary were going to miss the best part of the celebration.

Miss Norrie buttoned up the pink dress and painstakingly tied the bright yellow sash into another perfect bow. Cluck-clucking her tongue, she smoothed the gathers on the short sleeves and urged Martha not to roll around on the ground lest she ruin the delicate fabric.

Martha stared in disbelief at her governess— as if she were likely to throw herself down on the ground and roll like a saddle-weary horse! Sometimes she thought Miss Norrie did not understand her at all.

Stockings on, shoes on, fingernails examined—at last the long business of getting dressed was finished.

"There," cooed Miss Norrie, looking Martha over, "you look a picture, dear. Now if you'll just be a *good* lass and stay that way. . . ."

Her pale blue eyes squinched up with worry, showing clearly her doubt that Martha would manage to do so. Martha could not decide what she wanted most to do: force herself to keep as spotless as cousin Rachel, even if it meant standing stock-still the entire day—or run down the path and splash into Loch Caraid, just to stop Miss Norrie from *squinching* at her that way.

"Go and show your mother," Miss Norrie said,

and Martha went gladly out of the nursery.

Mum was in her bedchamber, looking out the window toward the loch. She was dressed for the wedding, too, her glossy brown hair piled high on her head in a mass of waves, with three fat curls hanging down over one shoulder. Everything about her seemed crisp and bright and new: the smooth silken expanse of her sun-colored gown, the snowy folds of lace on her breast, the shining round curls.

"Hullo, my lass, dinna you look lovely!" Mum greeted her, her smile shining upon Martha.

"Has the sun come out yet?" asked Martha eagerly, craning her head to see.

"Nay, not yet," said Mum. "But I've not given up hope. Sure and I've seen the light break through heavier clouds than this."

Martha leaned on her mother's knees and asked if she might run over to Nannie's cottage.

"I willna get in the way, I promise!" she begged, and Mum laughed.

"I ken better than that, Martha Morse—

you'll be ladling out the porridge before two minutes have gone by. But go on with you; and you may cross the loch and walk to the village with the wedding party, but you're to sit in your proper place in kirk, next to me, do you understand?"

"Aye!" Martha said, squeezing Mum hard and dashing down the stairs. She wondered if Miss Norrie would be as glad as she was that they need not cross Loch Caraid in the same boat.

Penny Wedding

As soon as she had stepped out the door, Martha forgot about Miss Norrie. For a minute she even forgot about Nannie's wedding, it felt so good to be outside. Even though the sun was not shining, it was a beautiful day. The whole sky was a mass of clouds. Some of them hung heavy over the mountains that rose up to the north and west behind the Stone House; those clouds were gray and thick. They were the clouds Martha had seen from the kitchen garden.

Above the loch, to the south, the clouds

were flat and airy white. A pale blue sky peeped out between them. The clouds were moving, sailing in the sky like boats skimming across water, and their edges shimmered golden. The sun was above them, wanting to shine through. The wind was helping; it was going to blow all those clouds from over the loch and the village beyond it, and bunch them up over the mountains where they could rain without ruining anyone's wedding day.

Martha closed her eyes and felt the wind on her face. She wanted to drink it. It smelled of heather and hay and clover honey. It was a moor wind, sweeping up the hill from the open land beyond the southeastern shore of the loch. It lapped the blue surface of the water and stirred up little waves there. It made the thin streams of smoke rising from the cottagers' houses lean sharply toward the mountains. On the hill between the little houses and the Stone House, the grass waved and rippled, just like the water. Everything was soft and green and rippling.

Martha wished, as she had wished a thousand thousand times in her life, that she could always live outside. Sometimes she thought she'd like to be a shepherd and live in the hills with her flock, with a warm plaid to wrap up in at night, the stars for candles, and a bed made of heather. But she knew she would never be allowed to spend even one night outside like the shepherds did. A laird's daughter could not be a shepherdess.

But she could be a wedding guest. She went a little way down the path toward the loch and the farmers' cottages. There were blue flags growing against the wall of Father's sheep barn, and she stopped to gather a bouquet of these for Nannie. She cut crossways over the grass to the cluster of thatched huts at the foot of the hill. One of them fairly shook with cries and laughter; that was Nannie's mother's hut, and it was crowded with well-wishers.

"Miss Martha!" cried Nannie, when Martha poked her head through the open doorway. Half the cottagers who lived on Father's estate were inside. Martha saw Mrs. Sandy, the wife of Father's steward, and Mrs. Tervish who lived next door to Mrs. Sandy, and Auld Mary who lived out on the moor. She saw Nannie's sisters and brothers and their mother, Mrs. Jenkins. Nannie was standing in the middle of the room in a snowy bleached-linen dress and her best blue-striped petticoat, having her golden hair brushed out long and smooth by Mollie, the Stone House housemaid. Mollie was a bridesmaid, along with Nannie's next-oldest sister, Helen, who worked as an upstairs maid in Martha's uncle's house.

"Come in!" Nannie cried out, waving at Martha. "Have ye come to break yer fast wi' us?"

Martha shook her head and said she'd already had her porridge.

"I brought you these," she said, holding out the flowers.

"Och, ye sweet lass," said Mrs. Jenkins. She took the flowers and set them on a table next to the fat bouquet Nannie's sisters had picked. "We'll add these to the bundle, dear."

Some of the guests were eating porridge and

others were drinking mugs of home-brewed ale. Mollie tied Nannie's hair in back with a pale pink ribbon and fastened another ribbon around her head with a bow in front. Then Nannie took out a silver ring Mum had lent her for the wedding.

"Och, I did tell the mistress over and over 'twas far too kind of her, but she said 'twould bring me luck. I must aye wear somethin' borrowed, to be sure—but this! I declare I'm that nervous I'll lose it, I canna spare time to be nervous about the weddin'!"

"Then Mrs. Morse has done ye a double boon, darlin'," said Auld Mary. "And I canna say it surprises me a bit. There's no a kinder soul in the glen than our Mrs. Morse."

Martha felt very proud, for Auld Mary was speaking of her mother.

Mrs. Jenkins stood staring at Nannie with tears in her eyes. "Och, if this isna the happiest day o' me life," she murmured. "And yet it tears at me heart to think o' me lass goin' away to live on the other side o' the loch."

Her voice was soft, so that Nannie did not hear her. But Martha could hear. She heard Auld Mary say in reply, "Aye, that do be the way o' weddins. Ye're sad an' happy all at once, and that's just as it should be. Ye've raised a lass to be prood o', Janet Jenkins, and she's marryin' a fine man. Sure and the sun will shine on them—ye'll see that I'm right."

Mrs. Jenkins took Auld Mary's hand and squeezed it. "It seems like yesterday ye were helpin' me at Nannie's birthin'. And here she is a grown woman, and me an auld lady, and ye—och, Auld Mary, ye're just the same as ivver ye were!"

Auld Mary cackled with laughter. "Aye, it's true," she said. "When ye're auld as the mountains, ye change just as slow."

Suddenly Nannie's youngest brother cried out from the open doorway. "A boat, a boat! Look there, on the loch!"

Everyone crowded to the doorway to watch the rowboat gliding across the loch toward them. Nannie's face went pale, and her cheeks were rose red.

"It's time," she whispered. "Och, I canna believe the day has come at last!"

"Will I have to call you Mrs. Cameron?" said Martha suddenly.

Nannie's laugh was like bells jingling. "I should think not! Sure and I'll be the same Nannie ye've kenned since ye was a wee thing!"

"Mrs. Cameron, Mrs. Cameron," teased Nannie's brothers and sisters.

The boat had reached the shore. Two young men were inside, dressed in Sunday clothes, and they leaped out, grinning widely, and strolled up the bank toward the cottage.

When they reached the door, they bowed deeply. Both men were cousins of Gerald Cameron; Martha knew them well from kirk. The one who spoke first was named Gerald Cameron, too, but he did not look anything like Nannie's Gerry.

"Does Miss Nan Jenkins live here?" he asked. Of course Martha knew he knew the answer, but those were the proper words to say. Since Nannie's father was dead, her mother answered in his place.

"Aye, what do ye want wi' her?" She pretended to be cross and suspicious. Everyone laughed; all of them knew the game and knew how it would turn out.

"We want her for Gerald Cameron," answered the groom's cousin. "Er—t'other one, that is."

Now the wedding guests laughed louder, and Mrs. Sandy called out jestingly, "Sure about that, are ye? Ye must look sharp in the kirk, Nannie, to be sure the minister weds ye to the right man!"

Nannie's face was red all over now, and her hands were pressed to her mouth to keep in the laughter.

"So ye want her for Gerald, do ye?" asked Mrs. Jenkins, going on with the game. "Well, ye canna have her."

"Then we'll take her!"

Mrs. Jenkins pretended to consider. "Will ye come in, and taste a mouthful o' ale till we see aboot it?"

The guests laughed and hurrahed and

clapped the two young men on the back as they made their swaggering entry into the house. Then Mrs. Jenkins took out mugs she had borrowed from the neighbors and poured drinks all around. There was toasting and jesting and laughter, and soon the two groomsmen went to Nannie and politely offered her an arm on each side. Blushing furiously, she hugged her mother and her sisters, and then she took hold of the groomsmen's arms and let them escort her out of the house. Martha waved and called out good-bye along with the others. Mollie and Helen hurried after Nannie and her escorts, and Nannie's mother and brothers came behind them.

Someone threw an old shoe toward the wedding party; it arced high above Nannie's head and fell with a splash into the loch. The guests hooted and hurrahed, but Nannie was careful not to look back. She must not look back once on her way to the kirk, or it would bring bad luck on her marriage—almost as much bad luck as rain would. But the clouds over the loch were stretching out as pale and gauzy as a fairy's veil, and the patches of blue sky between them were growing. The sun was going to shine on Nannie, Martha felt sure of it, and she knew that nothing would make Nannie look backward into the bad luck.

Martha wished she could ride in Nannie's boat, too, but she must cross the loch some other way. There wasn't enough room in cousin Gerald's boat for the whole wedding party, as it was. Nannie's mother and brothers climbed into a rowboat Father had lent for the occasion; it was Martha's brother Robbie's little boat, which was hardly ever used now that Robbie was away at school. Father preferred to send for the ferryman whenever he or Mum needed to cross the loch to get to the village or to Fairlie, for the ferryman's larger boat was far more comfortable.

Two or three other boats had been assembled to carry the other kirk-goers across to the village. Martha climbed into the one manned by Father's steward, Sandy. She settled onto the wooden plank seat with Sandy's small sons, Finlay and Donald, jostling on one side of her, and their sister Annie, who was just Martha's age, on the other. Another sister, Flora, who was six, sat opposite Annie beside their mother. Mrs. Sandy held the youngest Davis child, three-year-old Peggie, in an iron grip on her lap. Peggie protested loudly, but Mrs. Sandy said she was not about to let her bairn go tumbling into the loch.

"And that goes for ye lads, too," she added, eyeing Finlay and Donald sternly. "Sit still, mind!"

"Let's go! Let's go!" the boys cried, bouncing in their eagerness to be off.

"Let's go!" echoed Peggie.

"Do you think they'll have cake at the feast?" said Flora hopefully.

"Of course they will," said Mrs. Sandy.

Annie squeezed Martha's hand happily. A wedding day was a grand thing.

Just as Sandy was about to push off, a voice came careening down the hill: "Wait! Wait! Sure and ye've room for one more!"

It was Cook, and she was hurrying down the hill from the Stone House clutching a large basket to her breast. She had changed out of her usual brown-striped kitchen dress and stained linen apron into her good Sunday gown, an imposing garment of stiff gray linsey-woolsey with a lace-up bodice and a full, flowing skirt. The laces strained over her bosom as she pounded toward the shore. Gasping, Cook climbed into the boat and squeezed in between Martha and the boys.

"Och, to think ye nearly left me," she panted. "Had to wait for me pie to crisp, I did. I expect it's broken to pieces by now."

She lifted the cover of the basket and inspected her pie critically. A delicious nutmeg-and-cloves smell wafted out. There was the rich smell of roast meat, too, for Cook had brought the mutton legs she'd been roasting that morning, to contribute to the wedding feast.

"Eh, me pie looks well enough. A miracle, that," Cook pronounced. "I suppose I should have waited for the ferry wi' the master and missus. But I canna bear sailing wi' that Miss Norrie. She always carries on so."

"Here comes Shaw wi' the ferry now," said Sandy, gesturing across the loch with his chin, for his hands were busy pushing the oars as the boat slipped away from the shore.

"And there's his lairdship, comin' doon the hill," Mrs. Sandy added, pointing back toward the shore. "And Mrs. Morse and Miss Grisell—dinna they aye look a picture? Miss Grisie looks more like yer mither every day that passes, Miss Martha. Ye take after yer grandmither—yer father's mither, the auld laird's wife. A tall, spirited woman she was, and handsome enough, but not what ye'd call beautiful. Yer mither noo, she's lovelier than roses."

Annie squeezed Martha's hand again. Martha knew this squeeze was to say Annie was sorry her mother had said Martha was like the grandmother who was not beautiful. Martha didn't mind one bit. She liked Mrs. Sandy's frank way of saying things. Cook was like that, too. With them, you were not always left guessing about what a statement really meant, as you were about the things Miss

Norrie said. When Miss Norrie said you looked nice, she said it with worried eyes and wringing hands, so that you knew she was thinking something quite different—perhaps that she knew you would not go on looking nice for very long. Martha felt firmly that she would rather be told straight out a pretty frock was wasted on her, than have it be hinted at with wrinkled foreheads and anxious sighs.

She did not much care whether or not she was beautiful, either. It seemed to her that beauty took a great deal of effort. Mum and Grisie had to sit still so long each day, having their hair dressed by Mollie. Grisie spent hours and hours upon her clothes, embroidering and embellishing them, altering the shape of the sleeves, fussing with the bows. And then she had to go to great pains to keep them clean and neat. Grisie had not had time to visit with the cottagers, or watch the men at the haying, or help with the flax harvest, or do any such interesting thing, since she was a wee girl younger than Martha. She had never bounced one of the little Tervish babies on her knee and seen him laugh till his belly shook. She had never come in second in a footrace with the village children, as Martha herself had done just last week. To be sure, Grisie had never been scolded for coming home with her feet so muddy she had to be sent down to the loch to wash them before Mollie would allow her to set foot in the house. But what was a scolding compared with the thrill of having run faster than all of the girls and all but one of the boys! Only Lew Tucker, the blacksmith's son, had outrun Martha—and she had privately resolved to beat him, too, at the earliest opportunity.

Sitting squeezed in the boat between Annie and Cook, Martha had a feeling inside that was very like the feeling of running with the wind in your face and half the village at your heels. She turned around backward on her seat to watch Mum and Father and Grisie climbing into Mr. Shaw's boat, back at the shore. Miss Norrie was just behind them, wringing her handkerchief as she waited to be helped into the boat. It was no secret that Miss Norrie hated to be on the water. Martha watched them all grow smaller and smaller as the boat she was in pulled farther away from the shore. Mum and Grisie and Miss Norrie in their pretty gowns were bright specks of color, blue and rose and golden, like flowers on a distant hill. Against the blue water and the pale sky, the colors were so clear and bright they gave Martha an ache inside, sad and happy all at once. It was like what Nannie's mother had said about the wedding day.

The trip across the loch never took half as long as Martha would have liked. She loved the smell of the water, the cool kiss of the wind on her cheeks, the *plash-plash* of the oars cutting into the water. But today she did not mind when the boat reached the opposite shore. She could hear people singing; that was Nannie's wedding party, already landed and walking toward the village.

And there was a lovely surprise waiting on this side of the loch. As the boat bumped against the landing, the last of the cloud cover was swept away and the bright sun shone down like a blessing from heaven.

Martha and Annie and the other children ran to catch up with the wedding party. They trailed behind the bridesmaids, picking wild-flowers and singing the teasing, rollicking songs that were proper for a wedding-day morning. The boys called out jests to try to make Nannie look backward, but of course she did not let them trick her. All the way to the village Nannie was careful not to so much as turn her head to the side.

Clachan, the little village tucked between the various farms that made up Father's estate, lay some three miles from Loch Caraid. A well-trodden path meandered its way along-side the brook that flowed out of the loch here at its southern end. To the west, mist-green hills rose tall and steep against the sky.

After a while the brook path was joined by another path, slanting down from the South Loch farm, where Uncle Harry's family lived in the grand house called Fairlie. When the two paths met, the road grew wider, and that meant the village was not far off.

Martha looked for her cousins along the path, but she didn't see them. She supposed Uncle Harry had driven his carriage to the village. Mum said Uncle Harry would drive his carriage to the privy if he could. Uncle had been disappointed, after moving from Edinburgh to Glencaraid, to discover that the rough Highland roads made a carriage impractical. Most people walked wherever they had to go, or else they rode horses, if they had them. But Uncle Harry remained stubbornly loyal to his beautiful, shining, black-wheeled carriage. Mum said he spent fully half his time standing by the side of the road, waiting for his driver to dig the carriage out of the mud.

Mum could poke fun at Uncle Harry because he was her brother. Whenever Mum teased Uncle, Martha missed her own brothers more. She wished Perth were not so far away. Duncan had been away at school more than a year now. Martha wondered what he was doing right at that moment. Would he remember that today was the day of the wedding? Martha had written to tell him, but Miss

Norrie had said the letter was so blotchy and the writing so untidy that it would be a miracle if Duncan managed to read even a sentence.

The sound of bagpipes came soaring up the glen from behind Martha and the children; that was Sandy, piping for the bride. And every so often the music and chatter was startled by a *bang!* that echoed all around them—one of the groomsmen, firing a pistol into the air. That, too, was tradition.

They went across the small stone bridge, past the smithy and the weaver's shop, and there at last was the kirk. A crowd of wedding-goers milled about outside it. The groom's party was there already, for Gerald lived in town and had only to walk down the lane. Martha saw Lew Tucker, the boy who had beaten her in the race, and his friend Ian Cameron, who was one of Gerald's brothers. Ian was dressed in a stiff linen collar and a new jacket, and he looked as miserable as a cat in water. She saw her aunt and uncle and her cousins, and went to stand beside them.

Aunt Grisell gave her a kiss on the cheek, and cousin Meg said Martha looked pretty as a pink. Rachel and Mary, in their creamy white frocks, fairly dazzled Martha's eyes. She almost laughed aloud to think how anxious Miss Norrie would be if Mum ever chose to give her a dress as white as one of those dresses.

Martha saw Gerald's father, the village weaver, in the crowd, but Gerald himself was nowhere in sight. He was already in the kirk, of course, standing in front of the bridal pew. The groom must on no account lay eyes upon Nannie until she was led to her place by his side.

Soon Mum and Father and their party came to join the waiting crowd, and at last the groomsmen led Nannie inside. Martha pressed forward to get a look at her, but all she could see was the back of Nannie's golden head. Mum steered Martha toward the Morse family's pew. It was the best pew in the kirk, right up front across from the bridal pew, because Father was the laird. Martha was glad, for now she could see Nannie and Gerry very well. Gerry wore a new kilt of rich red-and-black tartan, and a red coat with a blue tartan sash over one shoulder. His broad, flushed face was proud and happy. He could not seem to take his eyes off his bride.

Uncle Harry's family filed into the row behind the Morses. Cousin Janet leaned forward to whisper to Grisie in front of her, and Grisie turned around to whisper back. Martha, sitting between Grisie and Miss Norrie, listened to them in amazement. They were talking about their own weddings. Janet whispered that she was going to have twelve bridesmaids, and Grisie said she would wear a gown of watered silk with pearls sewn into the bodice.

Martha snorted. To think of Grisie getting married! Miss Norrie stared at her in horror.

"Remember where you are, Miss Martha dear!" she whispered behind her fan. "Gracious!"

Martha wished she were still sitting with Annie and the Davises. But they were several rows back, with the rest of the cottagers.

The minister strode to the front of the kirk, his long black gown billowing around him. Martha craned her head past Miss Norrie to watch Nannie and Gerry. She wanted to see how they would change during the ceremony. They must be changed somehow. All the married people Martha could think of seemed very different from the unmarried ones. They seemed older, for one thing. Nannie did not seem old at all. Really she was not much older than Grisie.

That thought gave Martha a funny feeling inside. She could not imagine Grisie in Nannie's place, quietly radiant next to her groom. She could not imagine a young man staring at her sharp-tongued sister with eyes so joyous as Gerry's eyes. When she tried to picture it she could only see Gerry and Nannie.

The minister talked and talked, and Gerry said aye, he would take Nan Jenkins to be his wife, and Nannie said she'd take Gerald Cameron to be her husband. Then suddenly it was over, and Nannie was Mrs. Cameron now. Martha had watched like a hawk, but she had missed the moment of change. Whatever it was, it must be something that could not be seen. Nannie looked just the same; Gerry looked the same. Other people looked different, for many of the women were crying happily. Grisie and Janet were both sniffling behind their handkerchiefs. Mollie's eyes were shining in a way Martha had never seen them shine before, and Nannie's sister Helen looked as if she wanted to leap up and down and cheer.

The minister leaned forward for the kiss he was owed by the bride. Blushing, Nannie kissed him, and the congregation burst into a hullabaloo of cheering. Gerry paid the minister his sixpence fee, and the crowd filed out behind the newlyweds to head to the Camerons' house for the wedding feast.

Martha thought that walk was the noisiest, rowdiest, most delightful walk she had ever had in her life. As the crowd surged down the main street, Sandy and another piper blared out a lively song, and Lew Tucker's oldest brother played the fiddle. Sometimes the music could hardly be heard above the boom of pistol shots, and other times the piping was so loud Martha wondered if it could be heard clear on the other side of the mountains. She felt so sorry for Rachel and Mary and the other cousins, who had been ushered back into Uncle Harry's carriage and taken home to Fairlie.

All too soon the party arrived at Gerald's house. As they neared the house, a few of the young men and women struck up a race. Everyone knew that the first one to reach the house would be the next to marry. Nannie urged Mollie to run, and someone cried out that Miss Grisie ought to try. At that remark, Father pretended to glare sternly at the crowd, searching for the culprit. Everyone laughed, for they knew that on a wedding day, a great many jokes were allowed which would not be suitable at any other time.

"I dinna ken why ye didna try for the win, Margery Anne," teased Mrs. Sandy, elbowing Cook. Cook's mouth popped open and she stared at Mrs. Sandy with such indignation that Martha could hardly walk for laughing. It was so funny to think of sharp-tongued, red-faced Cook wreathed in bridal ribbons like Nannie.

"Go ahead and jest," retorted Cook huffily. "I'm sure ye wouldna ken it to look at me today, but I was the beauty of two parishes when I was a lass. Sure and there were a dozen lads who'd ha' given their right arms to marry me. Scamps and scoundrels, all o' them, and ye can be sure I sent them packin'. I vowed I'd nivver marry a man who loved me for my beauty only—and I suppose the good Lord took me at my word. If a suitor shows up today, at least I'll ken his heart's in the right place!"

Lew Tucker's brother was the first to reach the house. He had run with his fiddle in one hand and his bow in another. When he reached the threshold, he raised the fiddle to his chin and played a triumphant reel. Lew Tucker leaped in the air and cheered for his brother, which made everyone laugh. The Tuckers were known as a silent bunch. They were the fastest runners in the valley and the best blacksmiths in Glencaraid and beyond, so it was said; but the joke went that if ever two of them were to speak on the same day, the world would come to an end.

Gerald's mother came out of the house to welcome the bride. She had not gone to the wedding; she had had to stay home to prepare for the celebration. In her hands she held a large round oatcake, and when she held it up the guests cheered and hollered some more. Nannie stepped forward, blushing, with Gerald at her side. Mrs. Cameron held the oatcake over Nannie's head as Gerald led his bride across the threshold. Just as Nannie passed beneath the oatcake, Mrs. Cameron broke it in two. This was to welcome Nannie into the house and the family. Martha and the other children rushed forward to claim a morsel of the broken bread. Some of the older girls wrapped their bits carefully in handkerchiefs so that they might sleep with them under their pillows that night, in hopes of dreaming of their future husbands. Martha ate hers.

Then Mrs. Cameron took Nannie's hand

and led her to the hearth in the center of the wide main room. She picked up the fire tongs and put them gently into Nannie's hands. Nannie bent down and, with the tongs, adjusted the smoldering peats to make the fire burn brighter. Now she was really and truly a part of Gerald's family, and the cheers and well-wishing were deafening. Mrs. Cameron took up a shepherd's crook that had been brought inside for the occasion. She swung the crook over Nannie's head three times, saying solemnly, "In the name o' the Father, the Son, and the Holy Ghost, may the Almighty make this woman a good wife."

Now everyone was quiet for a moment. Nannie's eyes shone, and Gerald could not let go of her hands. Nannie's mother wiped her eyes and said, "Ah, me," in a voice that must have been louder than she meant, for she jumped and looked around in embarrassment. That set everyone laughing again, and it seemed to Martha that the laughing did not stop for the rest of the night.

There was only one thing left to do before

the dancing could begin. Nannie went to the meal barrel and pressed her hand into the ground oats as far as she could. The farther she pushed it in, the more luck it would bring her family. When she pulled her arm out, it was dusted with oat flour to the elbow. Gerald took hold of it and pulled her outside, and Lew Tucker's brother struck up another tune on his fiddle.

All the rest of that day and late into the evening, there was dancing and merrymaking in the Camerons' house, in their barn, and on the green grass in between. Nearly all the guests had brought along something to eat. Cook's pie disappeared in a matter of minutes, and her good roast mutton was pronounced the pride of Glencaraid. The food was part of Father's wedding present to Nannie. He also put a shilling into Gerald's hat when the hat was passed round for a collection. Each guest at the celebration put in a penny, and that was why it was called a penny wedding. But Father put in more than that, because he was the laird.

Mum, Father, Grisie, and Miss Norrie did not stay very long. But they said Martha might stay until the Davis children went home, if she promised to mind her manners and remember who she was.

Martha knew there was no danger of her ever forgetting that. She waved good-bye to her parents and sister. She waved to Miss Norrie, who looked at once relieved and tortured with worry to be leaving her charge behind in the care of Cook and the other cottagers. Then Martha ran to join the circle of children who were dancing in a ring around the bride and groom. She took hands with Annie on one side and Lew Tucker on the other, and she whirled and whirled while the trilling voices of the bagpipes soared above her and the fiddle wove its airy song in and out and all around her.

Copywork

With Nannie gone, Cook was very cross. She had no one to help her with the kitchen work: no one to peel the potatoes or to take a spell with the churn. Mollie was far too busy with upstairs work. Martha offered to help, but Miss Norrie would not allow it. Miss Norrie seemed horrified by the very idea. She set herself to thinking up new ways to occupy Martha, so that Martha would not feel she had so much free time that she could play at being kitchenmaid.

Martha knew this because Miss Norrie told her so, right out.

"We'll add an an extra half hour of practice at the pianoforte each afternoon—you're not coming on as quick as I'd like, you know—and I do think it's high time you received some instruction in dancing and comportment. Playing kitchenmaid, indeed! I should think you'd be grateful you were born above such things as peeling potatoes, Miss Martha!"

"When I'm grown up," said Martha stubbornly, "I shall peel potatoes every day if I feel like it. I'll hire a maid to play pianoforte for me, I will—and to wear my shoes and stockings, too!"

Miss Norrie's eyelashes fluttered in dismay, and Martha understood that she had been impertinent again. Her cheeks burned with shame. She could not seem to learn to think before she spoke. Mum said that was one of the most important lessons a person could learn—more important even than dancing and music and needlecraft.

"I beg your pardon," Martha said sincerely.

She meant what she had said about what she would do when she grew up, but she did not mean to upset Miss Norrie. She didn't like feeling naughty all the time. She had never felt that way until Miss Norrie came.

That afternoon, when Miss Norrie was lying down in the nursery to rest her nerves, Martha crept away from the hymn she was supposed to be transcribing into her copybook in the parlor. Every day Miss Norrie assigned an hour of copywork from a book of hymns. Martha thought the hymns themselves were rather interesting, but she did not like the tedious task of copying them, line by line, into her book. The ink got on her fingers and sometimes on her nose, which had a way of itching at just the wrong moment. The ink made pools on the paper, and Miss Norrie never seemed to leave Martha enough blotting paper to soak them up.

Leaving her quill sticking out of the inkwell, Martha went upstairs to Mum's room, where Mum and Grisie were busy at their sewing. They were laughing and talking together.

Martha stood in the doorway, staring at them. She felt outraged and lonely all at once. She wished she were a little girl of five or six years old again, allowed to run in and out of Mum's room or the kitchen as she pleased.

Before Miss Norrie came, Mum had been the one to teach her things. Mum had taught Martha to spin and to sew and to read. Grisie had taught her to knit, and she had not been cross about it, either. She had been patient and encouraging. Grisie was always nicest when she was showing Martha how to do something that she herself did very well.

"Martha!" cried Mum, breaking into her thoughts. "I didna see you there, lass, you were so quiet."

"She must be ill," teased Grisie, and then her eyes met Martha's and her brow furrowed with concern. "Mercy, I was only teasing, but happen it isna so funny. Look, Mother, how red her cheeks are!"

"I'm not ill," said Martha in a choking voice. Then words burst out of her before she knew they were going to. "Mummy, why must I

48

have a governess? Canna you and Grisie teach me yourselves? Grisie plays the pianoforte so beautifully, and her stitchery is ten times lovelier than Miss Norrie's—"

"Whisht, Martha, hold your tongue! Suppose she hears you, child!" Mum looked worriedly past Martha to see whether Miss Norrie might be hovering a few steps behind in the hallway.

Martha came into the room and ran to sit on the little footstool at Mum's feet. "Nay, she's sleeping, and you canna hear what anyone says in here from inside that old bed in the nursery. I should ken, for I've tried."

Mum and Grisie looked at each other and broke into laughter.

"I've nay doubt you have," said Mum wryly.

"She's right, too," added Grisie. "I remember I used to try to stay awake to see if you and Father were talking about me. But I never could hear anything except Alisdair's snores."

"And Cook's snores," put in Martha. "They come up through the floor."

Grisie laughed again. "Aye, I'd forgotten

that. I canna hear her from the new room. I suppose it's lucky for me Father gave me the chamber in the front part o' the house, for if I'd the back part, my bed would be right over Cook's bed, wouldna it? And my new bed hasna the walls yours has to muffle the sound."

"Oh, me," Mum laughed, shaking her head. "You lasses are terrible. But Martha," and now Mum's eyes grew serious, "what's this about not wanting a governess? Dinna you like Miss Norrie? She's a fine teacher and wonderfully patient."

"I suppose . . ." said Martha softly. She did not know how to explain that there was more than one kind of patient. There was patient like Mum, who always seemed as though showing you how to do something was the most delightful thing she had ever done in her life, no matter how many mistakes you made while you were learning it. And there was fluttering, murmuring, hand-wringing patient like Miss Norrie, who said things like, "Don't fret, dear, I'll sit here all night if I must," and "There now, I'm sure a clever lass like you can figure it out if you'll only put your mind to it." Miss Norrie's patience announced itself; Mum's just *was*.

Martha gave up searching for a way to explain it and said stubbornly, "I'd rather have you for a teacher, or Grisie."

Mum's voice was very gentle. "Grisie's a young lady now, Martha. She has a great many obligations. And I've a household to run—and you might not believe it, but there are things Miss Norrie is better qualified to teach you than I am. It's been a long time since I seriously studied music, or drawing, or grammar. Miss Norrie came to us very highly recommended by the headmistress of your cousin Janet's school in Edinburgh. She's a very intelligent young woman, you ken."

"And she's a brilliant seamstress," said Grisie. "Kens all the latest fashions, she does."

"But," Martha said doggedly—she was not trying to be stubborn, but she could tell by the slight frown on her mother's face that she was sounding that way—"I dinna care two

beans for fashions. Nor for drawing, or wax-
work, or dancing, or all that. If I have to study
something I'd far rather study Latin and geog-
raphy, like the boys are doing at school. Latin
is useful, at least; so many books are written
in it."

"Latin?" shrieked Grisie in disbelief.
"Latin's a dead language, Martha, for scholars and lawyers and such. It's not as though
you can sit down and have a *conversation* in
it, for pity's sake."

"But I could have conversations with the
scholars and lawyers," retorted Martha, "if I'd
read the same books they had."

"Girls, girls, that's quite enough," said
Mum. "Goodness. Really, Martha, I'm quite
at a loss here. You must have a governess, and
that's all there is to it. Your father and I fear
we allowed you to run wild far too long as it
is. You're a headstrong girl, and a reckless one.
Miss Norrie is exactly the sort of meek and
gentle person from whom you can learn a great
deal, my lass. That's why I engaged her."

By now Mum had resumed her sewing, her

needle making its calm dives into the creamy linen fabric on her lap. Martha was quiet for a moment, and the room was quiet. She watched the bottom ruffle of her mother's gown rise and fall a tiny bit with each of Mum's stitches. The ruffle was a deep green color, a shade darker than the rest of the gown. Its tiny folds and pleats were perfectly spaced, and the stitches were invisible. Martha remembered that Mum had made that gown a year ago. She had begun it late in the summer and was finished early in harvest time. One week Martha had been allowed to go out and watch the flax harvest, and every evening when she came back to the Stone House, Mum had sewn a little more of the ruffle. The flax harvest and the ruffle had each taken three days to complete.

When at last Martha spoke, her voice was very small.

"She doesna like me. Miss Norrie, I mean."

"What?" Mum looked up from her sewing, eyebrows raised high. "Why, Martha lass, whatever makes you say that? Miss Norrie's quite fond o' you, she's said so many a time! And how could she not be? You're a dear, sweet, stouthearted lass who does her duty with a right good will when she sets her mind to it."

"And your handwriting is improving," added Grisie encouragingly, sounding so grown-up that Martha gave a little involuntary shudder. "I saw your copybook, and really the last few pages are almost legible!"

Martha made a face at her sister. Perfect handwriting, like all the other things Miss Norrie was striving to teach her, took a lot of time to accomplish. And all the while you were working at it, you knew that you were missing the really important things happening on the estate. Fish were being caught, jam was being made, hay was being mown, rabbits were being chased—and you were stuck inside at the table, writing row after row of little black words.

"Oh!" gasped Martha suddenly, remembering the book, the quill, the jar of ink she had abandoned in the parlor. "My copywork—I must finish before—"

She did not wait to complete the sentence. Pounding down the stairs, she smelled caraway and cloves and knew that Cook was making a seedcake for tomorrow's dinner. All the mixing would be done by the time Martha was free to join her, but perhaps Cook would save the bowl for her to lick.

Bundling the Flax

Martha missed the haymaking that year. She could not remember a year in her life when she had not been allowed to run out to the meadow and watch the cottagers at work with their scythes, whisking off the hay in great sweeping strokes. Both men and women swung the scythes, and their children came along behind gathering the fallen stalks into bundles and stacking the bundles on end in the stubbly field.

Last year Martha had helped with the bundling. This year the haymaking was over before she knew it had begun. Miss Norrie kept her so busy with lessons that she had little time left over for playing outside. Every day there seemed to be some new accomplishment Martha must master: how to wash lace without ruining it, or how to paint enamel, or how to make tassels and fringes and twisted silken cords. One morning Martha looked out the nursery window and saw the rows of yellow hayshocks in the field beyond the barns, and her heart gave a little flip. Summer was running away, and she was missing the best part of it.

The thought came to her suddenly that Miss Norrie had grown up in a town. Perhaps the governess had never seen hay being mown! Perhaps she did not know how exciting it was, with the scythes swinging and each worker racing to finish his row before the others, and little bits of hay working their way inside everyone's clothes and making them wriggle and scratch in a crazy sort of dance.

The more Martha thought about it, the more it made sense. Miss Norrie was like her cousins

Rachel and Mary had been, when they first came to live at Fairlie. They, too, had never seen a haymaking, or a flax harvest, or a wool-waulking, or a sheepshearing. Martha had wanted to show them all these things. But Aunt Grisell did not like her little girls to run loose in the fields. She would not let them roam about their own South Loch estate, much less Father's big Glencaraid farm on this side of the loch. When the cousins came to visit at the Stone House, Miss Norrie supervised quiet picnics in the garden and gave extra dancing lessons, for she said it was good for Martha to practice with partners her own size.

But if Miss Norrie had never seen a harvest—then of course she could not be expected to understand what was so marvelous about it.

All the time these thoughts were going through her head, Martha had been standing at the parlor window, staring out. Beyond the shorn hay meadow was a sheet of blue as blue as the loch; that was the flax meadow, and the sky-colored flowers meant it was ready to harvest. Martha turned away from the window and ran to where Miss Norrie sat frowning over an inkstain on the dress Martha had worn the day before.

"Miss Norrie! You *must* go, you must come with me and see what it's like—"

"Gracious, Miss Martha! Do leave off clutching my arm like that, dear; you'll shake me to pieces," said Miss Norrie crossly. "I must come and see what? Have you spilled your porridge? I suppose it's run all over your embroidery; I *have* told you, dear, not to leave your things lying about on the table—"

"Nay, nay, that isna it," Martha said, laughing and exasperated. "I did put me stitchery away—"

"*My* stitchery, Martha; mind your grammar."

"*My* stitchery, then," gasped Martha. "Miss Norrie, may I go watch the flax being harvested, and will you come with me? We'll have a grand time, I swear it."

Miss Norrie's eyebrows soared upward in horror. "You must never swear anything, Martha; it's dreadfully wrong! Oh, dear, just when I begin to think we've made some progress . . ."

"Beg pardon," said Martha hastily. She did not care how much Miss Norrie scolded, if only she said yes. "Might we go, then? It's only across the meadow and the burn, and the burn's so narrow there we can leap right over it—you needna worry about getting your shoes wet."

"Leap over a brook? My gracious, Martha, I don't know what's gotten into you this morning! We cannot leave our lessons to go off cavorting in the fields and leaping over brooks like a pair of sheep! What would your mother say?"

"I dinna ken. Let's ask her," said Martha, and before Miss Norrie could close the startled O of her mouth, Martha was racing upstairs toward her mother's room.

Mum listened to the gasped-out request, and she looked over Martha's shoulder at Miss Norrie, who had come swiftly into Mum's room behind her pupil. Then Mum looked at Martha, and her eyes seemed to be studying Martha's face as if they saw words written there.

"Methinks," said Mum after a long silence, "there is little that Miss Norrie wishes less to do than to go and stand in the hot sun watching the workers perspire. But"—she went on, while Martha's heart was plummeting within her—"I do think, lass, 'twould do you good to take in some fresh air for a change. Sure and you've been looking rather peaked of late. Go on with you, only mind you keep out of the farmers' way, and do what Mrs. Sandy tells you. Miss Norrie, you may consider today a holiday. Happen you'd like to go for a nice row on the loch? I can get Sandy to take you."

Miss Norrie shuddered. "Oh, no, madam, I'm sure that isn't necessary. I—er—thank you—I shall endeavor to use my free time fruitfully. . . ."

Her voice dropped to a whisper, as if Martha were in the next room instead of standing right beside. "Only . . . do you think it's quite the best thing for the child to be unsupervised in the fields? Of course I'll go along to take care of her, if that's your wish, madam—"

Mum laughed. "Heavens, nay. Martha will

be quite all right. Sure and she'll get into less mischief in the fields than she does here at home!"

Martha ran to her mother and threw her arms around her.

"Och, thank you, Mum! I'll be good as gold, see if I'm not."

"I'll settle for good as silver, lass."

How lovely it felt to be outside! Martha jumped onto the louping-on stone that her father stepped on to get on and off his horse. All around her the grass was bright with thistle and clover. A great noise of laughter and talk floated up from the loch, and when Martha looked down the hill she saw that Mr. Shaw's ferryboat had just reached the shore. It was full of people from the village, most of them children. Every year villagers came across to help bring in the flax crop. Father paid by the bundle, and many of the village parents let their lads and lasses out of home chores for a day or two so that they might bring home a few extra pennies.

"Hallo!" Martha called, waving to them

from the path. She hurried toward the boat, although she knew she'd have to turn right around and walk back up the hill to get to the flax field.

The children surged out of the boat and moved forward in a noisy, jostling crowd. The ferryman's own daughters, Una and Betty, were among them. Martha saw Ian Cameron and Lew Tucker and the miller's three children. All of them were glad to see Martha. When she was younger, Martha had spent many an afternoon playing games on the hillsides or at the lake shore with the sons and daughters of her father's tenants, and the children of the villagers. It had not mattered then that she was the laird's lass.

In the clamor of greeting, Martha had not noticed the last person to step onto shore. She did not notice that person until she fell into step beside her and Martha turned to see a familiar rosy-cheeked face beaming at her.

"Nannie!" cried Martha, stopping dead in her tracks. She halted so suddenly that Una Shaw bumped into her and Lew Tucker bumped into Una. Lew laughed and begged Una's pardon, and then Martha said it wasn't Una's fault and begged both their pardon.

Nannie giggled and said, "Och, Miss Martha, I've missed ye."

"You've come for the harvest?" Martha asked.

Nannie said she had. She said she hardly knew what to do with herself these days, now that she had only her own small cottage to take care of and just two mouths to feed. "Feel like a great lady, I do, sittin' on me duff half the day. The house is so new there's hardly any cleanin' needs doin', and I've made my funeral clothes and Gerald's both. Me mither said that's a wife's first duty, and Gerald brought home some fine woolen cloth that was his share o' the weavin' for Mrs. Biggins. So the death-clothes are made an' safely stored away (and may it be a good many years afore either o' us needs them), and the berries are no ripe yet for jam, and I've swept the floor sae many times Gerry says we'll soon be steppin' down when we come into the house! This mornin' he says to me, he does, 'Nan, my lass, I hear the laird is wantin' help bringin' in his flax. I suppose yer mither and the young ones will be after earnin' their coppers? Happen ye should take the ferry over and catch up on the news from the north side o' the loch.' I fairly flew out o' me chair, I was that excited. And here I am!"

By this time the group had passed the barns and the mains, a long turf building that housed any unmarried men who worked for Father. The children and Nannie strode through the stubbly hay meadow, where some of those men were loading the shocks of hay into a cart to be hauled to the barns for storage. As Martha and the others drew near the low stretch of land that Father had planted in flax, they heard a cheerful noise of song. The flax harvesters were singing as they worked.

I have heard the skylark singing
His love song to the morn.
I have seen the dewdrop clinging
To the rose just newly born.

But a sweeter song has cheered me,
At the ev'ning's gentle close,
And I've seen an eye still brighter
Than the dewdrop on the rose.

'Twas thy voice, my gentle Mary,
And thine artless winning smile,
That made this world an Eden,
Bonny Mary of Argyll.

Martha sang, too, as she came near to the workers. Sweat poured down their faces as they stooped and straightened, moving along the rows of flax. The sun was warm and the wind seemed to have worn itself out on the hills before it reached the field, for there was no breeze.

The blue flowers at the top of each flax stalk were bright and cheerful. When Martha stared out across the unharvested rows, the wide stretch of blue looked as cool as Loch Caraid. She stood a moment, watching the bending backs and moving stalks. It was like a dance. No one missed a step.

Bundling the Flax

Flax was not cut with a scythe, like hay. The tall stalks had to be pulled up by the roots in handfuls. That was the part the grown-ups did. It was strenuous work, hard on the backs of the men and women who stooped over the flax, row after row. But singing made the work go faster. The harvesters yanked up the stalks and threw them down in time to the music.

Nannie went quickly to stand beside her mother. Mrs. Jenkins straightened up in surprise and hugged Nannie and said she was looking well. Mrs. Sandy and the other women at work in the field called out greetings also. Mr. Gavin Tervish asked her teasingly if her husband knew she'd run away back to mother. Nannie laughed and answered, "Run away! Why, sure and didna he *send* me!"

The harvesters burst out laughing, and then, as if on a signal, they all turned back to their work. Nannie took up a place next to her mother and bent to pull out a handful of the tall stalks. The song soared back above the field.

Tho' thy voice may lose its sweetness
And thine eye its brightness, too,
Tho' thy step may lack its fleetness,
And thy hair its sunny hue,

Still to me wilt thou be dearer
Than all the world shall own.
I have loved thee for thy beauty,
But not for that alone.

Martha and the other newcomers ran to join the children who were already there. The children's job was the same as with haymaking: gathering the pulled stalks and tying them into bundles. Each of them piled the bundles into heaps along the margins of the field, making sure to keep the heaps separate. At the end of the day, Mr. Tervish would count the bundles, and Father would come with a purse full of pennies to distribute to those who'd earned them.

Martha had never bundled flax before but she had watched it being done many times.

She ran to find a pile of fallen stalks, and she gathered them together into a neat sheaf. Then she realized that she had not thought to bring any string. She looked around at the other children who had all come prepared with balls of string or coarse thread in their pockets. They were working busily, without looking up. Flax-bundling was a sort of contest to see who would go home with the most pennies. The children of the Glencaraid cottagers, who had had a head start because they had not had to cross the loch, had already collected many bundles each. The village children were biting off strings and bundling as fast as they could to catch up.

Desperately Martha searched the pockets of her apron in hopes of finding a stray ball of string, though she knew none was there. She did not like to ask the others to share theirs. If she asked anyone, that child would feel bound to share, and then perhaps he would not have enough string for his own bundles. That would not be fair, for Martha had only come to help for fun. The others had come to help put bread on their families' tables.

There was nothing in her pockets except a folded strip of linen: a sash Miss Norrie was making her embroider. Martha's fingers felt the linen and the small soft skeins of silken thread Mum had given her for the embroidery. The thread was very fine and strong. It had come all the way from Perth, for Father had brought it home as a present for Mum after his last trip to the city.

Martha stood staring at the bright skeins of thread. She had not yet used very much thread from either color; so far she had only finished the border at one end of the sash. One of the skeins was as golden as Nannie's hair, and the other was cherry red.

Ian Cameron saw her standing frozen in the middle of the field and called out teasingly, "I thought ye came to help!" In a flash Martha had made up her mind. She shoved the sash and the skein of red thread back into her pocket. Using her teeth, she broke off a piece of the yellow thread, and she knelt to wrap it around her bundle of flax stalks.

The thread was so fine that she wrapped it several times around so it wouldn't break. Then she knotted it tightly and took up the bundle. All the other stalks in her row had been bundled and piled already. She tossed her bundle a little way away from one of the piles and ran to find more fallen stalks.

It was hard work, bundling. The flax stalks were scratchy and they cut into Martha's hands. Sometimes she did not wrap her thread around tightly enough, and then the stalks slid out of the bundle when she picked it up. She watched Una Shaw and saw how Una used her knee to hold the string tight while she knotted it. Martha tried to do the same thing. She had to concentrate so hard that she could not sing along with the other workers, and for a while she hardly heard the singing.

But she was very happy. Her pile of bundles grew into a small hill. It was smaller than the piles around it, but that didn't matter. She did not expect to win the contest; she only wanted to do a respectable job.

The yellow thread ran out, so she started on the red. Her bundles, tied with the fine silken thread, looked fancy next to the other children's. Martha wished they looked the same. She did not want anyone to think she gave herself airs because she was the laird's daughter and had silken thread instead of plain string.

Then the red thread ran out, too, and she had to stop. Her hill of bundles could grow no taller. But it was a hill, at least, and she supposed it was not fair to take away too many bundles from the others. For the first time she wondered if Father would give her pennies, too. She felt a pang of doubt; if she had not come to help, perhaps Una or Ian or Lew would have had that many more pennies to take home that evening.

When she had thought that, she was almost glad she had run out of thread. But she was glad, too, in a different part of herself, that she had made *some* bundles at least. If Father offered her any coins, she would ask him instead to buy her some sweets the next time he went to Perth, and then she would share them with the children.

Mrs. Sandy stopped pulling stalks and stretched her back. Loudly she announced that it was time for dinner. Indeed, the noon-time sun burned hot overhead, and Martha's shadow was small at her feet.

The workers straightened up and wiped the sweat from their foreheads. Lazily they strolled to a spot at the edge of the field where a little burn burbled past on its way to Loch Caraid, and a thicket of alder trees shaded its green banks. Someone had tied a jug of whey to one of the trees and left it floating in the burn to keep it cool. The jug was passed round, and the women took out bulging napkins which, when unfolded, revealed thick slices of bread with bacon between them, or bannocks and wedges of cheese.

"Has yer mither found a lass to take me place in the kitchen?" Nannie asked Martha, settling herself on the grass near the cool water.

"Not yet," Martha said, sitting down beside her and accepting a fat slice of cheese from Mrs. Sandy. "And Cook's that cross about it you canna imagine."

"Nay, I can well imagine it," said Nannie, shuddering. Then she laughed and said, "Och, I must say me own dear wee kitchen seems terrible quiet, wi'out Cook there grumblin' and fussin' and tellin' her stories. I keep catchin' meself turnin' around to ask her what she'd like me to do next!"

Mrs. Jenkins chuckled over her bannock. "Ye'll grow used to bein' mistress o' yer own kitchen soon enough. But when the bairns start comin', ye'll wish ye had a kitchenmaid o' yer own!"

Nannie's merry laugh bubbled out. "Och aye, when Gerry earns his fortune, I shall be a great lady, and I'll hire me an army o' maids—ye shall be one, Annie Davis, and Una and Betty and—"

"I want to be one, too!" cried Martha. That

made everyone laugh. Mrs. Sandy's whole body shook with laughing.

"Och, Miss Martha, ye'll worrit yer poor mither to death one o' these days, wi' yer wild notions. Imagine the laird's daughter sweepin' ashes and shellin' peas in a weaver's kitchen! Ye'll marry an earl, most likely, or a duke, and ye'll be the one wi' the army o' scullery maids."

Martha tossed her head. "Pah! I wouldna want to marry some old earl. In the stories they're always cross and nasty, or else all they do is hunt. I'd rather marry someone who does something interesting with his days. I could help him." She looked at Nannie. "I might marry a weaver's son myself. I'd like to work one of those big looms."

"Hear that, Ian?" said Lew Tucker wryly. He was grinning at Martha, and when the others caught the joke they again burst into uproarious laughter. Martha felt her cheeks burning. She had not been thinking of Ian when she said she'd like to marry the son of a weaver. Ian was laughing and looking embarrassed all at once, and Lew's eyes were twinkling.

If Lew Tucker could tease her, she could tease him back. She gave another careless toss of her head. "I said 'I might.' Who kens, I might just decide to marry a blacksmith instead. He'd be handy to have around when I needed an iron kettle or some such."

Then everyone laughed again. The joke was on Lew now, for he was a blacksmith's son.

"Speaking o' kettles, Martha," asked Mrs. Sandy seriously, "are ye certain they willna be missin' ye at dinner? I dinna suppose yer mither gave ye leave to spend all day oot here wi' us?"

Martha gasped and jumped to her feet. She had not thought to ask. Of course Mum would expect her home for the midday meal. That was the most important meal of the day, and she had never before been allowed to miss it.

"Una, you can finish my cheese!" she cried, leaping over the burn and running swiftly as a sheep dog across the shorn hay meadow.

A Lesson Learned

She was late for dinner. Cook tsk-tsked as Martha splashed her hands and face in the kitchen basin, and Father's face was stern when Martha came hurrying to the table in Mum and Father's bedroom, drying her hands on her skirt. Mum looked at Martha with disappointed eyes. Grisie was polite enough to pretend to take no notice; she went on taking dainty bites of bread, her eyes fixed upon her plate. But Miss Norrie's whole being was trembling with dismay. She half stood, scraping her chair on the floorboards, her hands twisting her napkin tight as a cord.

"We've all been waiting—I'm sure I feel partly to blame, though I *did* think you were old enough to observe the simplest rules of propriety. I suppose I ought to have gone to fetch you myself—oh, dear, how disgraceful!"

By now the governess had turned toward Father and was wringing her napkin at him instead. "Nothing of the kind has ever happened with a child under my tutelage before, I assure you—"

"Yes, Norrie, so you've been telling us," said Father dryly. "They must have been quite a remarkable bunch of children, your previous pupils."

Grisie made a smothered sound and quickly brought her own napkin to her face. Martha, slipping into her seat beside her older sister, stared hard at Grisie. She had a suspicion that Grisie was actually laughing behind the striped cloth.

"Remarkable indeed," said Mum softly, spearing a steamed oyster with her fork. "Not a one of them ever late to table, you say. How very impressive."

Miss Norrie nodded eagerly. "They *were* impressive children. Wonderfully well behaved, and the girls so sweet tempered and quiet. How it *did* tear at my heart to bid them farewell. They are in France now, as you know."

"Aye," said Father, "so you said."

He laid his knife upon his plate and looked once more at Martha. His eyes were gray as pewter. She could not tell what he was thinking. Across the table from Martha, Miss Norrie had grown silent and was now engaged in smoothing her napkin upon her lap.

"Martha," said Father, turning his eyes suddenly back to Miss Norrie, "is the fifth child in this house to arrive at table *after* the meal had begun. Yes, Grisie, even you," he said, for Grisie had given a little gasp of surprise. "Though happen you were sae young you canna remember it. Your brother Robbie was late more times than I could count, the summer we gave him the rowboat. At last I told him I'd take the boat back and give it to one o' my men to go fishin' in. I dinna think he was ivver tardy again, after that."

"Alisdair was the worst, though," said Mum. "When I think how many times I had to send someone looking for that lad, while the rest o' us were finishing our soup and moving on to the meat! Got so caught up in whatever he was reading, he did, that he'd have missed dinner altogether and been none the wiser if Grisie hadna dragged him to table."

"I had to snatch the book away," said Grisie. "That was the only way to get his attention."

Martha was laughing now. She loved to hear about the naughty things her older brothers and sister had done when they were little. It was reassuring to know she was not the only Morse child who had ever done something to deserve one of Father's stern looks—or worse, one of Mum's disappointed ones.

But Father raised his eyebrows at her and said it didn't matter if a fault was a common one among children; it was still a fault and must be taken seriously. "Though I willna quite call it a fault, when you've only been late for dinner the one time. Still, Martha, if tardiness for dinner is what comes o' allowing you a free morning to go out and play, then happen you're not deserving o' that liberty."

"Aye, Father," said Martha meekly. She wanted to look away but didn't dare take her eyes off Father's. "I was helping with the flax, and when the others sat down for dinner, I didna think about coming home. I just sat down and ate with them."

"'I didna think' is your most common excuse, Miss Martha," interjected Miss Norrie. "You simply *must* learn to think once in a while."

Father frowned, and Mum regarded Miss Norrie with serious eyes.

"I think we've heard enough on this subject today," Father said. "Next time Martha is given a free day, she'll not forget her duty."

He picked up his spoon and returned to his broth. Inside herself Martha sighed with relief. She felt a great deal like the fish she had often seen wriggling at the end of the fishermen's lines. Sometimes when a fish was small, it was held dangling in the air, its round mouth opening and closing silently, while the men discussed whether it was worth keeping or not. Martha understood now how the fish must feel when at last the shrugging fisherman had released it from the hook and tossed it back into the cool blue water.

After dinner Father went out to look at the oats in the north field. Grisie disappeared into the parlor, and soon the sound of pianoforte music came tinkling up the stairs. As Mollie cleared the dishes, Mum went to her writing table and opened her account book. She took up her quill and sat quietly making little tick marks next to entries in the book. Martha went to stand behind her. She liked to see the rows of household items:

Ink ready-made, 1 bottle at 11 1/2 d.
Lamp oil, 1 anker (in trade to peddler for cask of ale)
Claret wine, 10 bottles at 14d. the bottle
Brass pan from peddler, 3 shillings

A Lesson Learned

Miss Norrie had remained at the table, staring out the window while Mollie leaned around her to reach her dishes. But after a moment she stirred herself, sighed, and said she supposed Martha had better have her lessons now.

"Although they do say it's a terrible strain on one's brain to work so soon after eating," she added fretfully. "You ought properly to spend a suitable period of time in rest, to allow for good digestion."

"Truly?" asked Martha, interested. "But what about the people picking flax or bringing in the hay? They have to eat fast and then go right back to work, or the rain might come and ruin the crop before they get it in. And Mrs. Sandy says her whole family is healthy as horses."

At the table dishes clinked in Mollie's hand, and her mouth was quirking up at the corners. Miss Norrie frowned at Martha and said, "I'm sure they are, if Mrs. Sandy says so. I suppose she is well read on matters of medical science?"

Mum looked up sharply, her pen suddenly

stilled. Something in Miss Norrie's tone made Martha wonder if she had been impertinent yet again. But it was so funny to think of Mrs. Sandy poring over scholarly journals that she couldn't help laughing.

"Och, o' course not!" she replied, shaking her hair back off her shoulders. "I dinna think Mrs. Sandy even kens how to read. But she kens a great deal about things just the same. Mum says there's not a wiser soul in all the glen, except Auld Mary—dinna you, Mum?"

"Aye," said Mum softly, giving Miss Norrie a curious stare, "I do."

Miss Norrie flushed and looked at the floor. "Ah, well then. I'm sure I didn't mean . . ." She cleared her throat. "Nevertheless, one must draw a distinction between the constitutions of the gentry and those of the, er, working classes." Her eyes flicked uncomfortably toward Mollie, who was taking a much longer time than usual removing the dishes from the table. Mum had put down her pen altogether and was listening to Miss Norrie with folded hands and uplifted eyebrows. Something in her expression seemed to make the governess nervous, for Miss Norrie suddenly clapped her hands together in a bright sort of way and turned to Martha with a wide and brittle smile.

"Now then, dear, we mustn't stand here chattering while the day runs away from us. Let's hie us to the nursery and see how your sash is coming along."

Martha gasped, remembering suddenly. She wondered what Mum would say about her having used the good silk thread to tie flax bundles. She knew beyond a doubt what Miss Norrie would say. Mollie left the room with her tray full of dishes, humming softly to herself. Martha wished she could follow her. She would far rather help do the washing in the kitchen than have to confess what she was going to have to confess now.

"I used up the thread," she said. She felt somehow it would be better to get it out all at once and be punished than to go on feeling this dreadful anticipation of the scolding that must come. "The red and the yellow. I used it to tie the flax. I hadna any string to wrap the bundles, you see."

"Och, Martha!" cried Mum in dismay. Miss Norrie's eyes were wide open with astonishment and horror.

"The silken thread?" she whispered. "That lovely silken—why, my gracious, that thread must have cost more than a month of my wages. How could you, you naughty, thoughtless child! I declare, I've never heard of a child doing something so very wicked—"

"Norrie!" said Mum sharply. "That is quite enough. You may leave us. I shall deal with Martha myself."

Miss Norrie's mouth opened and closed. The fleeting thought ran through Martha's mind that now Miss Norrie was the one who was like a fish. With quick steps the governess left the room.

Martha stood before her mother, waiting. Mum was quiet for a long time. First she stared at the closed door and then she stared at Martha. Her eyes were very blue and sad.

Martha felt a terrible ache in her heart. She hated to disappoint Mum.

At last Mum spoke.

"Martha, I have two things to say to you."
Her voice was low and firm, and Martha found
she had to struggle to keep looking her mother
in the eye.

"The first thing," Mum continued, "is that
I owe you an apology."

This was so unexpected that Martha actually jumped in surprise. She stared at Mum
in astonishment. Mum chuckled and put a
hand to Martha's cheek.

"Do you think your mother never makes a
mistake, lass? Sure and we're all human here.
Martha, you were right. Miss Norrie doesna
like you."

Martha was more surprised still. She had
felt that in her bones for some time, but it
was nonetheless a jolt to hear her mother say
it out loud.

"You mustna brood about why she doesna,"
Mum said gently. "Sometimes one person cannot understand another. Miss Norrie thinks
she understands you very well, and that's
where the trouble lies. She doesna ken what

kind of person you are *really*, not the slightest bit. She only thinks she does. And that means she is not at all suited to be your governess. I shall dismiss her this afternoon."

Martha could only blink. There were too many surprises swirling around in her mind to allow words to come out. Miss Norrie was going away. Thinking of that made a strange kind of lump come into her throat. It was something like a crying lump, but she did not exactly feel like crying. She felt more like playing the pianoforte very loudly.

Mum went on speaking in her gentle voice. "Miss Norrie was right in saying that what you did with the thread was naughty and thoughtless. But she was very wrong to say it was wicked. Wicked is doing wrong on purpose. And I must say, lass, that of all the naughty things I have known you to do in your eight and a half years—" Her eyes twinkled, and she added, "And to be sure there have been a great many of them—I am hard pressed to come up with a single thing among them which you did with purpose or malice.

Your great fault is thoughtlessness, Martha. But you have always shown yourself willing to do what is right. When you have learned to ask yourself *before* you do anything whether it is right or not—then you'll not find yourself in naughty scrapes all the time. Do you understand what I am telling you?"

"Aye," Martha murmured. "I didna think about the thread at all. I just found it in my pocket and I used it. I'm awfully sorry, Mummy."

"I ken, lass," said Mum. "And that was the second thing I was going to tell you—that *you* owe *me* an apology. You've just made it, and I forgive you. But you must work to make right what you've set wrong. Miss Norrie may have overstated a bit when she spoke of how expensive that silk was. But it did cost a great deal— far more than your father ought to have spent on me. I allowed you to use it because I thought it was time you had something truly fine to wear of your own making. 'Twould have been a lovely sash, Martha, and 'tis a shame you'll have to finish it with plain linen thread. And your penance shall be doing so without a complaint and working as hard as ever you can to make it nice."

The shame burned in Martha's chest. She had not known Mum had given her the silk thread as a special treat. She had only felt grumbly about having to use it, because Miss Norrie had fussed over each stitch so much. Now she understood that Miss Norrie had been anxious to help her make the sash as beautiful as possible.

"Och, Mum, I'm so very sorry!" she said again, throwing herself into her mother's arms. Mum stroked her hair, laughing.

"Hush, now, lass. Go to the nursery and ask Miss Norrie's pardon, too, for spoiling the sash."

Martha nodded, swallowing.

"And then," Mum continued, "run down to the kitchen to see Cook for a while. Miss Norrie and I have things to discuss."

Cat, Mouse,
and Hedgehog

The next morning Sandy carried Miss Norrie's baggage down to the loch and loaded it into Robbie's boat. Upstairs in the parlor, Miss Norrie brushed Martha's hair for the last time and then they told each other good-bye. Miss Norrie was going home to her father's house in Edinburgh. She sniffed a little and said she would miss Martha dreadfully. But Martha did not think Miss Norrie really meant it. That was the polite sort of thing people said during good-byes.

Martha felt as though she ought to say something similar, to be polite herself. But she couldn't, for that would be lying. She was not going to miss Miss Norrie at all. She could hardly wait for her to go. Her scalp still stung from the hair brushing. She thought happily that perhaps Grisie would brush her hair tomorrow.

Martha watched from the top of the stairs as Mum shook Miss Norrie's hand and wished her good fortune. Grisie came to stand beside Martha. She whispered to Martha that Miss Norrie had told her she was secretly relieved to have an excuse to leave. The governess had not liked living so far from any town; she had only taken the post because her friend Miss Caldwell recommended it. But living on the village side of the loch, Miss Caldwell got to see a great deal more of society than Miss Norrie had. There was always a stream of visitors coming and going from Uncle Harry's house.

"I canna say I blame her," Grisie murmured in Martha's ear. "It's so quiet and dull here on our side. No one ever comes to call."

The door closed behind Miss Norrie, and Mum turned to come upstairs.

"Of course they do!" replied Martha indignantly. "Laird Alroch comes, and the cousins, and Auld Mary's down in the kitchen with Cook this very minute!"

Grisie rolled her eyes heavenward. "Auld Mary's a dear, but she's not exactly society, Martha!"

Mum, arriving at the landing, laughed merrily.

"Och, aye, Grisie, sure and we ken the kind o' society you mean. You're thinking o' the dances and parties your Aunt Grisell likes to give. I never saw such a lass for dancing as you!"

Grisie looked sheepish. She followed Mum into the big bedchamber, Martha tagging along behind.

Grisie said, "We've hardly the space here for dancing even if anyone *did* live on this side of the loch. How can Father stand it, owning half the valley and living in a house nearly as small as a farmer's cottage?"

Mum sat down in her sewing chair and cocked an eyebrow at Grisie. "You'd not find it so small if you actually had to spend any time in a real cottage. Do you really think this house is the same as all of us sleeping and cooking in one room together, with the cattle looking over the wall, like in the Tervishes' house, or the Davises'?"

Grisie bit her lip, ashamed. Martha stared openmouthed, for her sister never did anything to merit a scolding. Grisie went to Mum's writing table and fiddled with the quill that stuck upright from the inkwell.

"May I have some paper, Mother?" she asked. "I'd like to write Janet."

Mum smiled. "Aye, it's been a whole day since your cousins have heard from you. They'll be worrying." She unfolded a wide sheet of linen cloth upon her lap. "Here, Martha, help me spread this over the footstool. There's a tear at the foot of the sheet here. Your father *will* keep forgetting to cut his toenails."

Her mother made a wry face, and Martha laughed. She felt very happy. She couldn't decide what she wanted most to do: to spend the morning with Mum and Grisie, listening to their funny conversations and helping Mum with the mending, or to run downstairs and find out what Auld Mary had come to see Cook about. In the end curiosity won out. After she had spotted the small rip at one end of the bedsheet, she begged to be allowed to go to the kitchen. Mum smiled and said she was surprised it had taken Martha so long to ask.

"Tell Auld Mary I've some wool I'd like dyed, if she's the time to do it," Mum said. "I'm wanting a fair bit o' crimson for suit coats for your brothers. No one brings off a red dye like Auld Mary."

Martha hurried downstairs. Cook stood before the long table in the middle of the kitchen, slicing turnips into a bowl and telling Auld Mary a story that was making the old herb-woman cackle. Auld Mary sat on a bench near the hearth, a reed basket on her lap and her withered hands bent over the handle, laughing till her shoulders shook. Hedgie, awake for once, was snuffling around on the ground near Auld Mary's hem.

"Aye, and when they went to count 'em at the end o' the day," Cook said, chuckling, "there were her bundles tied up pretty as you please, like a heap o' Hogmanay presents!"

"Eh, and here's the wee miss herself," cackled Auld Mary, wiping her eyes. "So, Mouse, I hear ye've been getting yerself into a fine big scrape, and chased yer governess away in the bargain!"

"I didna chase her—" Martha began indignantly, but then she saw how Auld Mary's eyes were twinkling at her.

"Ye're the Mouse that chased the cat away," Auld Mary teased. She had nicknamed Martha "Mouse" a long time ago. If any of Martha's brothers had ever tried to call her Mouse, Martha would have kicked him. But she liked it very much when Auld Mary said it.

"Good riddance, I say," said Cook with a snort. "I never much cared for that Miss Norrie. Too high-steppin' to pass a how-do-ye-do wi' a cook or a housemaid—and herself no better than a paid servant like the rest o' us!"

Auld Mary waggled a bony finger at Cook. "Whisht, ye'll do the Mouse nae favors by teachin' her to speak ill o' her elders. From what I could tell, that Norrie lass was a well-meanin' soul wi' a silly head and weak nerves. She wasna a bad sort, only a poor hand wi' children."

Auld Mary was so old that even grown-up ladies like Miss Norrie were "lasses" to her.

Martha watched how Cook pursed her lips and nodded her head, thinking over Auld Mary's words. No one but Auld Mary could scold Cook and get away with it.

"Ye're right as always, Auld Mary," said Cook, digging out a rotten spot of turnip with the point of her knife. "But I'll not pretend I'm heartbroken she's gone. Our Martha deserves a governess wi' a bit more spirit, that's

what. I hope the mistress has better luck wi'
the next one."

Martha picked Hedgie up, mindful of his
quills, and let him nuzzle her face with his
pointed nose. She climbed onto the high stool
beside Cook and filched a piece of raw turnip
out of the bowl. She shared it with Hedgie,
savoring the crisp, sharp flavor, but all the time
her mind was racing. Of course there must be
a "next one." Miss Norrie's going had been
so sudden that Martha had not thought, yet,
about the new governess that would come to
take her place. Perhaps she would be worse
than Miss Norrie.

Martha finished the bit of turnip and
reached for another one. Cook batted her hand
away from the bowl, but then she cut a nice
fat slice of turnip and gave it to Martha right
off the knife.

"Noo then," said Auld Mary suddenly, in a
different kind of voice. "I've got that ointment ye wanted here in me basket, Cook. Put
it on mornin' and night for seven days runnin',
startin' on the morrow, when the moon will

be full. Ye'll find it takes yer warts away quick enough."

Cook thanked Auld Mary and took the small crock of ointment from the old woman. She put it carefully on a shelf in the dish cupboard and returned to her slicing.

Auld Mary said to Martha, "I suppose, Mouse, that yer fine lady mither will be wantin' some wool dyed one o' these soon days?"

Martha choked on her turnip. "How did you ken it?" she asked, gaping at the wrinkled old woman. "Asked me to tell you that very thing, she did!"

Auld Mary laughed and laughed. She did not say how she knew. She knew things; that was Auld Mary.

"Mum said she'll want a good bit o' crimson," said Martha. "For school clothes for me brothers. I dinna ken what else."

Auld Mary nodded and said that was fine, as she had on hand a good bit of the lichen that brought out the rich red color Mum wanted.

"It wants soakin' a week or two in a pot o' home brew," Auld Mary said. "Tell yer mither I'll be ready for the wool any day after the new moon. Ye ought to come along and help, if she gives ye leave, Mouse," she added. "I canna imagine she'll have found ye a new cat that soon."

Martha jumped off her stool, startling Hedgie into spreading his quills. Gingerly she soothed him and set him on the floor, where he looked up at her with his glittering black eyes. She grinned at the hedgehog. Mum must let her go help Auld Mary, she *must*. She had never helped dye wool before. She had seen Mollie and Nannie do it, but they had always ordered Martha to keep well away from the cauldron of boiling dye. Martha was older now; Auld Mary said she was old enough to help. Martha danced about the kitchen in excitement.

"Mind yer bouncin'!" Cook scolded. "Would ye have me cut off a finger?"

"Och, nivver!" Martha said, throwing her arms around Cook's waist and squeezing. Cook squawked and made a show of holding her knife high in the air where it couldn't hurt anyone, but she couldn't help smiling at Martha. Martha hugged Auld Mary, too, and then she turned to run upstairs. She had just remembered her embroidery; she thought perhaps she would try to get a good bit of it done before she asked Mum if she could go to the wool dyeing.

The Cauldron on the Moor

Mum's big bundle of wool was too heavy for Martha to carry. Sandy walked with her, the three washed fleeces flung over his shoulder, to Auld Mary's hut on the moor beyond the steep jutting hill known as the Creag. Mum wanted two full fleeces dyed red for spinning into sturdy woolen yarn, and she had sent the extra wool to be dyed different colors on another day. Auld Mary could get a beautiful golden yellow

color from heather flowers, though other women in the valley said they had tried many
times and it was simply not possible. Most yellow dye had to be made with saffron threads,
which came from faraway India and cost a great
deal of money. Only Auld Mary could get
yellow for free, from the fragrant pink heather
that was so plentiful on the hillsides all around.
Auld Mary knew all the secrets of flower and
leaf, root and lichen. Mum said Auld Mary had
lived so long on the moor among the heather
and the gorse that it was a wonder the old
woman hadn't sprouted leaves herself.

Sandy tramped steadily along, humming a
low rambling tune to himself. Martha walked
beside him, picking handfuls of the tiny white-
fringed flowers that were scattered among the
wet grass. The day was clear and humid; a
great bank of fog hung low over the loch
beneath a soft gray sky. Martha looked out
across the water and wondered what her
cousins were doing in their grand house on
the other side. A swift soared over her head,
slicing the sky with its long, curved wings. It

swooped and dove, darting after some insect too small for Martha to see. She liked the way the swift screamed and shrieked as it flew. No one hushed a swift, and it would not listen if someone did.

As they were crossing the grassy shoulders of the Creag, some of the Davis children came panting up behind them, calling for Sandy. Mrs. Sandy had sent them with a message for Auld Mary.

"Flora burned herself and it's raised a fearful blister," said Annie, gasping. "Mither is wanting some hyacinth root to soothe it."

"Ye'll have to come along and fetch it home yerself," said Sandy. "I'm no goin' directly home, but takin' the long way round by Henry Gow's hoose."

Annie clapped her hands joyfully, and she fell into step beside Martha. Finlay and Donald raced ahead across the rough grass, weaving a path between the gorse bushes. The tall mound of the Creag sloped upward behind them. Martha turned back to look for the jutting gray shapes of the old stone wall on its peak. She had not climbed the Creag all summer, for Miss Norrie had thought it too dangerous a place for a young lady to play. Martha half feared that the ancient, crumbling wall that stood atop the lonely hill might have crumbled away altogether while she wasn't looking. But she could see the old wall standing there just as it always had. It made Martha feel very old herself, thinking of how long it had been since she had climbed that wall.

Auld Mary's hut lay a good distance beyond the Creag, out on the open moor. This was the eastern edge of the valley, and purple-gray hills rose up beneath the pale sky far in the distance. All the country in between was an empty, rolling, treeless plain carpeted with bracken and heather and gorse. In all the mournful Gaelic songs that Mollie liked to sing as she worked, the moor was a sad and lonely place; but today, with the heather glowing rosy purple and the gorse branches rippling in the wind, Auld Mary's moor was as bright and cheerful as a garden. All around, the birds were busily twitting and chirruping. A pair of

skylarks wheeled overhead, pouring their lilt-
ing song into the wind.

Annie murmured to Martha that she wished
she too could stay at Auld Mary's and help
with the dyeing.

"But Mum is makin' soap at home," she
said wistfully, "and she'll be needin' me to
help wi' the bairn, and to get dinner on."

"You can get dinner all by yourself?" cried
Martha, impressed. "I wouldna ken how. Anyway, I'd never be allowed."

"Why should ye have to?" Annie asked, her
eyes crinkling at Martha in bewilderment.
"Ye've got a cook to save you all that bother."

Martha could not think how to explain without complaining. She looked at Annie and
noticed for the first time how differently they
were dressed. Annie's frock was a plain, faded,
blue-and-white striped linen. Next to Martha's
bright green-and-gold tartan, Annie's stripes
looked like two dull shades of gray. Martha
had a wide satin hair ribbon to match her
dress, while Annie's hair was tied back with

a bit of coarse black thread. Annie's hands were red and rough, with dirt under the nails. Martha sometimes had dirt under her nails, but it was not from doing housework. When they were clean, her hands were smooth and white, like Mum's and Grisie's.

Ever since she could remember, Martha had run and played in the hills with Annie and the other cottager children. They had made houses in the birch groves, with hazelnut shells for fairy dishes. They had waded in the burn and gotten themselves soaking wet trying to leap across it. They had played Babylon and jack-straws and pirates.

But this past year she had played with them less and less. Annie had a great many chores to do; she was Sandy's oldest child and had to help her mother with the little ones. Una and Lewis and Ian and the other village children could not get leave to come and play on this side of the loch very often anymore. They, too, must stay home to help their parents. And then of course the boys had school. Martha didn't know if Una went to school anymore. Annie seldom did; she was too badly needed at home.

Martha looked at Annie again and felt her insides swirl with the strangest mixture of pity and envy. Annie had to work very hard, harder than Martha did; Mrs. Sandy could never spare Annie for an entire day of freedom on the moor. But then, Annie was *needed*. There was no one, really, who needed Martha's help. Mum could just as easily spot the tear in a sheet all by herself. Cook could get dinner on with Martha's help or without it. When Martha did help her, it was only because Cook had searched for some little task that Martha could do without making too much of a mess.

And yet there was Annie, the same age as Martha, cooking meals for her whole big family all on her own.

"Why do ye keep starin' at me like that?" Annie demanded, her sun-browned face breaking into a wide grin. "Have I porridge on me nose?"

"Nay—" Martha began, but she did not

know how to explain. "Look, there's Auld Mary's house."

The little turf hut rose up from the heather like a fat brown mushroom. Auld Mary was out in front of it, laying strips of dried peat on a fire that was built in a cleared patch of soil. There was a ring of stones around the cleared patch, sooty and stained with ash. Two stout wooden poles with forks at their top ends stood on either side of the stones. A third pole was laid across the forks, making a rail to hang a kettle. A great iron cauldron sat on the ground near the fire.

Auld Mary straightened her bent back and raised a hand to greet the children and Sandy. Her rough gray hair was tucked beneath a red kerchief, and her black eyes sparkled.

"And here ye are just in time to hang me kettle for me," she said, chuckling. "Me auld back will thank ye for it, Sandy Davis. Sure and I can cure anything exceptin' auld age."

She gestured for Sandy to lay the fleeces on the clean and springy grass. He lifted the huge kettle above the fire and hooked its handle over a sturdy iron hook that hung down from the rail. Martha heard something sloshing inside, and a sharp odor assaulted the heathery air.

Auld Mary nodded in satisfaction and offered Sandy a "wee drop o' drink" to stay his thirst before he turned for home. But Sandy shook his head and said he couldn't stay.

"And mind ye dinna stay too long yerselves," he called to Annie and the boys as he struck back out across the moor. "Ye mustna go worritin' Auld Mary while she's about her work."

"Whisht! As if such a pack o' bright-eyes could worrit the likes o' me!" laughed Auld Mary. "Brought the whole tribe wi' ye today, have ye, Mouse?"

"I wish they could stay," Martha said. "Annie says she must go home."

Annie nodded. She told Auld Mary about the hyacinth root, and Auld Mary went bustling into the dim hut to get it for her. An orange cat put its head out the doorway and looked at the children; Martha bent down, holding out her hand, and the cat trotted toward her with its tail upright. Annie's brothers crept forward to peek into the dark opening of the hut. Then suddenly they jumped backward, for Auld Mary had caught them peeking. The auld herb-woman chuckled and put a hand on Finlay's head. Annie laughed at her brothers for behaving as if Auld Mary's house were some mysterious cave of secrets. It was only a turf hut of the most everyday sort, and no one lived there but Auld Mary and the cat.

But Martha knew just how Finlay and Donald felt. She had believed Auld Mary's cottage was a place of mystery and secrets, too, when she was their age. She still felt that way, a little. She knew, for she had visited many a time, that inside that hut were shelves and shelves of potions and tonics and ointments. There were pots of paint and little carved wooden people, for Auld Mary made dolls sometimes as presents for the children in the glen. There were roots and bundles of herbs and old birds' nests. Every cranny held something wonderful to look at, and Auld

Mary had a story for everything there.

The old woman gave Annie a parcel made up of a faded cloth napkin tied around something small and lumpy. From one of her apron pockets the old woman took out four crisp round bannocks and passed one to each of the children. Then Annie and the boys said goodbye and struck back out toward the loch and home. The boys did not run and whoop and holler this time, for they were eating their bannocks.

"Noo then, we'd better get doon to it," said Auld Mary, taking up a long smooth stick that had been leaning against the side of the hut. Martha felt suddenly very grown-up. She and Auld Mary were left alone to do their work, with the orange cat and the wind and the skylarks for company.

Whatever was inside the black kettle was beginning to give off steam. It did not smell at all nice.

"What is it?" Martha asked, and Auld Mary said it was the lichen still soaking in the home brew. Martha wrinkled her nose. She knew what "home brew" meant; that was a delicate name for something that was not the least bit delicate. It was *graith*—the water you passed into the chamberpot at night when the house was closed up and you could not go outside to the privy. If you saved the graith and kept it in a warm place for a week or two, that was home brew.

"Faugh!" She shuddered and asked Auld Mary why the graith didn't turn wool yellow instead of red.

Auld Mary laughed. "It's the lichen what brings aboot the red, lassie. The home brew only helps the lichen do its work, and keeps the color from runnin' back out later. Aye, it's said the Lord works in mysterious ways, and I reckon this be one o' them. There's good tae be found in most ever'thing, if ye ken where to look."

Holding her breath against the smell and taking care not to drop her bannock into the graith, Martha stood on tiptoe to peek into the cauldron. She could see dark flecks of lichen swirling in the brew as Auld Mary stirred with the long stick. Then the old woman took up one of Mum's fleeces and put it carefully into the pot. The soft white wool sank down into the brew, little fingers of red liquid soaking into it as it settled heavily to the bottom. Auld Mary pushed at the fleece with her long stick, making sure every bit of it was covered by the dye.

"Noo we must wait and watch," she told Martha.

Martha munched her bannock and thought about the dye. There were a great many mysteries swirling in that cauldron. She had so many questions for Auld Mary that she could not wait till the bannock was swallowed to ask them, but instead spoke around the savory oatcake as best she could and felt thankful her mother was not there to see her poor manners. Who had first thought to scrape old lichens off a rock or a tree and put them to soak in a chamberpot? What would make *anyone* think that would result in something useful—much less a beautiful dye for wool or linen? And why did the lichens, which were gray-green in color when you saw them on rocks, make a crimson dye, while purple-pink heather flowers bloomed yellow in the dye pot?

One of the best things about Auld Mary was that she had answers for nearly every question, and if she did not have an answer, she had a story that served almost as well. The very best thing about her was that she never minded the questions, no matter how many there were, nor made remarks about your tongue falling off if you didn't give it a rest. While she pushed the sodden fleece around the dye pot with her stick, she told Martha all sorts of secrets about dyes and mordants and herbs. She said the secrets were so old that even the loch was young when this knowledge was new.

"Ye canna stint on the home brew, for that's yer mordant, that makes the color fast," she said, "Wi'oot it, yer nice red wool will fade to a plain gray after it dries. And ye've got to let the graith sit for a good long spell first—nae less than a week, and better longer. Ye can mix bog mud wi' graith to get a nice glossy black, and o' course iv'ryone kens that boilin' woad leaves in the home brew gives blue.

"But ye'll no want to use graith in every dye. There's all kinds o' mordants, just as there's all kinds o' dyes. There's wood ashes, or alder chips, or burnt kelp if ye live on the coast. Alum is good fer gettin' a good fast blue oot of elderberries, if ye have the pennies to buy it, and ye'll get a nice green from privet berries an' leaves the same way. But ye can do nearly as well wi' fir club moss if ye ken just when to pick it. Ye've got to use the right mordant fer the right dyestuff, or all ye'll come oot wi' is a grand mess."

"How ever did you learn it all?" Martha asked, breaking off a bit of her bannock for the orange cat, who had come to twine itself around her legs in the friendliest manner. She felt awed by how much Auld Mary knew. She had always known Auld Mary was very wise and learned, for all she had never spent a day at lessons in her life, but it seemed impossible that anyone could remember so much about dye plants and still have room for knowledge of any other sort. And yet dyeing was only one of the things Auld Mary was expert in. She was a healer, too, and everyone in the valley came to her for herbal tonics and cures. Mum said Auld Mary was better than a whole college of doctors.

"I've lived a long time and made a great many mistakes," said the old woman, her eyes twinkling. "The trick is tae remember yer mistakes and learn from 'em. After a while ye get auld enough that ye begin tae run oot o' new ones tae make."

She lifted a bit of the wool out of the dye to see how the color was coming along. It was a deep rosy red: nearly done, but not there yet.

The excitement of seeing the dye work its magic, and the clean heathery wind sweeping across the moor, and the thrill of having a cat think well enough of you that he curled himself into a ball right on top of your left foot and closed his eyes for a nap—all of it made Martha feel very bold and alive.

"Och, Auld Mary," she asked eagerly, "will you teach me everything you ken? I want to ken everything about—everything! Herbs and dyes and cats and birthin' bairns and all the important things in the world."

Auld Mary threw back her head and laughed and laughed.

"All the important things, eh? Ye and me, Mouse, we're cut o' the same cloth. Aye, let's us see if yer mither will give ye leave tae come back tomorrow, and I'll show ye how tae get that nice sunny yeller oot of heather. Ye've got to pick the flowers right when the sun's comin' up, that's aye the secret. And noo it's time we were gettin' that fleece oot o' the pot."

When the Cat's Away

I t took time to locate a governess who was willing to accept a post in such a remote location as Glencaraid. The autumn weeks slipped quickly past, and so long as Martha worked steadily each morning on her sewing, her knitting, and her lessons, Mum allowed her the afternoons free to play and roam and help Auld Mary. So Martha stitched and studied with all her might; she toiled at the embroidered sash with a diligence that would have pleased even Miss Norrie; she took pains over her copywork and learned to write out an entire hymn without more than three or four blots. She worked so doggedly on the stockings she was knitting as a Hogmanay present for Duncan that before she had quite realized it, the left stocking was nearly long enough to fit Father. Grisie teased her about that, but Martha only tossed her head and unraveled the stitches. She liked pulling out knitting, anyway; it was great fun to see the loops of yarn pop-pop-popping out of their neat rows as she pulled.

All the time she had the thought in the back of her mind that if only she showed Mum how good and hardworking she could be, Mum would forget about governesses altogether. It was so lovely not to have someone looking over her shoulder all the time or fretting when she came home of an evening with dirty feet. Every afternoon when Mollie cleared the dinner plates from the table and served the sugared cream and fruit and nuts that Cook had prepared for dessert, Martha felt a happy jumping in her blood. The end of dinner meant she was finished being a young lady until suppertime.

On rainy days she spent the afternoons in the kitchen with Cook and Hedgie. The little hedgehog soon learned that if he roused himself from his heavy slumber, there would be a nice bit of cheese or bacon waiting for him in Martha's hand. Martha sat cuddling the drowsy hedgehog on her apron and watched Cook mix and knead and scrub and sweep. While Cook worked she told Martha stories about fairies and kelpies and the fair seal-people who lived in the ocean and once a year came ashore to shed their sealskins and dance on human legs beneath the moon. Sometimes Cook let Martha help with the cooking. When the apples were ripe, Martha helped Cook prepare them for drying, and there were plums and currants and pears to stew and store in jars for winter meals. There were jams and jellies to make, and cucumbers to preserve, and eggs to pickle. Autumn was a busy time in the kitchen, even on wet afternoons.

When the sun shone, Martha stopped in the kitchen only long enough to fill her apron pockets with nuts and raisins or a handful of cookies, if Cook would let her have any. Then she dashed outside. Every day when she burst out of the house, she felt as though she had wings. The swift and the lark were her cousins; they soared on the wind above Father's estate and she soared upon the grass and through the fields. She knew every inch of the Glencaraid farm. She knew where the sheep were being pastured each day, and which of the tenants were harvesting turnips and which were sowing the west field in winter rye. She knew which of the barn cats had had a late litter of kittens, and it was Martha who discovered that the black sheepdog with the white ears and muzzle had split open its paw on a broken alder branch.

She visited a distant pool where the rows and rows of flax stalks were being soaked to separate the long fibers so they could be heckled and spun. But she did not visit it often, for the rotting stalks smelled very bad. It was another mystery that such foul-smelling plant stems could be turned into clean linen thread. Soon would come the hecklers, the band of traveling men who set up camp in a shed on Father's property each year and combed the long flax fibers smooth with their many-toothed heckling brushes. Then Mum and Grisie and Mollie and Cook and all the other women in Glencaraid would spin and spin and spin until all that loose fiber was turned into skeins of yarn.

Some days she went to the cottages to see what the women there were doing. But usually the mothers and the girls her age were working too hard to have time to visit. Martha always offered to help with the washing or the preserving, but the mothers looked at her with scandalized eyes and said they should think not. So Martha ran to the Creag, to see if anyone was playing there.

Usually there was someone. Annie Davis was often sent outside with her small brothers and sisters, to keep them out of mischief while Mrs. Sandy did her chores. Martha helped Annie mind them. Keeping the Davis boys out of mischief was no easy task. They were always trying to leap over gorse bushes or jump into the loch. Usually they fell into the bushes instead, and then they had to be fished out with great care lest their clothes be torn to shreds. No one, not even Finlay or Donald, wanted to face Mrs. Sandy with ripped trousers. But they never *really* jumped in the loch. That was only their way of teasing Annie.

The little Davis girls liked to play games, like Babylon and Merry-Ma-Tanzie. Annie said she was getting too big for such games, but Peggie and Flora begged her to play, so she did. Martha didn't care whether she was getting too big or not. They all clasped hands and went around in a circle, chanting,

Here we go round the mulberry bush,
The mulberry bush, the mulberry bush.
Here we go round the mulberry bush,
And round the merry-ma-tanzie!

Then they dropped hands and everyone pretended to move a broom back and forth over the ground, as they sang,

This is the way we sweep the floor,
Sweep the floor, sweep the floor,
This is the way we sweep the floor.
And round the merry-ma-tanzie.

This is the way we wash the clothes,
Wash the clothes . . .

Little Peggie was very funny to watch at the pantomime; the others laughed and clapped for her as she hiked up her skirt and petticoat and pretended to stomp upon a heap of clothes in a washtub. Martha wished she had a little sister at home, or a small brother—especially a roguish one like Finlay or Donald.

The very best afternoons were those she spent with Auld Mary. Autumn was a busy time for the old herb-woman; she roamed all over moor and mountain to harvest the leaves and berries and roots she used for her medicines and dyestuffs. She showed Martha where the bilberries grew fattest, and how to dig pignuts and wild carrots for a tasty snack. She taught her how to use cornflower petals to cure mouth sores, and how to make an ointment out of hedge mustard that would soothe rheumatism and cure jaundice. Martha drank in the secrets like water.

One cool, bright day Martha met Auld Mary on the path beside the loch. Auld Mary said she was going to walk up the near slope of Ben Fallon to gather fallen elder branches there. Mum did not mind where Martha went, if she was with Auld Mary. So Martha walked along beside the old woman, up the steep green slope to where the elder trees grew. Auld Mary called them bour-trees. Beneath their branches mushrooms squatted in friendly clumps, and tree pipits sang *chew-chew-chew* from the branches. Auld Mary and Martha picked up as many fallen twigs as they could find—it was terribly unlucky to cut or break an elder branch—and Auld Mary told Martha how every part of the tree, from bark to twig to berry, held some of the healing magic that made it a treasure to the sick folk of the valley.

"In the spring ye want the blossoms fer treatin' sores and burns and such like, and also fer headache and measles and the scarlet fever," Auld Mary said. "And then the leaves will soothe a sprain or clear a stuffed nose. The bark and the root are good fer a weak heart, and I've oft used bour-tree bark to cure the shaking fits that plague the Jenkins lad so terrible."

"That's real magic, I think," said Martha. "Making people well. That's better even than the fairy magic in stories."

Auld Mary smiled her crinkly smile. "Puts me in mind o' the tale about the golden bour-tree, it does."

"Och, tell it, tell it!" Martha begged.

So Auld Mary told it.

Auld Mary's Tale o' the Lass, the Wool, and the Golden Bour-Tree

There once was a poor widow who had three daughters, and each o' them was bonnier than the last. They lived in a glen at the foot o' a great green mountain all covered wi' bour-trees and brambles. At the top o' the mountain there lived a giant, and a terrible fearsome creature he was said to be, wi' three ugly heads and a nasty temper. But as he nivver came doon from his mountaintop, and the widow and her daughters nivver went all the way up to the top, the giant gave them nae trouble.

One day, however, the widow fell ill, and wi' the last o' her strength she whispered to her daughters that the only thing 'twould cure her was the bark o' a golden bour-tree. Now there were a great many bour-trees growin' on the mountainside, but none o' them were what ye might call golden. They were naught but the common, everyday sort o' bour-tree. The lassies kenned o' any number o' ailments the bark o' a common bour-tree would cure, but that was no what their mither had asked fer.

The only golden bour-tree the lassies had ivver heard tell o' was one that grew, so 'twas said, in the garden o' the giant at the top o' the mountain. The lassies, they were that worrited they didna ken what to do. They dared not go up the mountain to ask fer bark from the giant's bour-tree, fer they feared he'd as soon gobble them up as look at them. But they dared not stay away, either, fer their dear mither lay dyin' fer want o' that bark!

At last the eldest daughter summoned her courage and said she would go. She wrapped up in her warm shawl and set off up the mountain, climbin' past the brambles and past the common brown-trunked and green-leaved bour-trees. She climbed right to the top o' the mountain, where the gray stones rose in steep crags and the auld eagle wheeled about in the gray sky overhead. There before her was a great high wall made o' stones as dark as blood, and just o'er the top o' it, the lass could see golden leaves rustlin' in the wind. 'Twas the giant's garden, and there was the golden bour-tree just on t'other side o' the wall.

The lass stood starin', but she dared go no further. She covered her face wi' her hands and wept, fer she feared her mither must die.

"What have ye to weep aboot, lass?" croaked a strange voice, and the lass started in fright. She looked all aboot her, but nivver a soul did she see.

"Who spoke?" she cried oot.

"Who else?" answered the voice, and it sounded as if it came from over her head. The lass looked up, and sure there was the auld eagle, wheelin' above her. He gave one mighty flap o' his wings and came to perch on a stout juniper branch nearby.

"What ails ye, then?" the eagle asked in his rasping voice. The lass poured oot all her troubles—how she needed the bark o' the golden bour-tree to save her mither, but she feared the giant would eat her up if she went and asked him fer it.

The eagle spread his wings and flapped them. "I've a notion," it said. "Suppose I were to fly into the garden and tear off a bit o' the golden bark wi' me talons. I could be in and oot in a minute, and the giant would be none the wiser."

"Och aye!" cried the lass, thinkin' this a grand notion. "Will ye do that fer me? Please, I beg ye!"

But with those words the eagle reared back his head and screamed a loud, shrill scream. Right away a door opened in the giant's garden wall, and oot came the giant himself, as terrible and ugly a creature as the lass had feared he might be. He stomped to the lass and snatched her up in one hand. Every one o' his three heads wore a fierce, glowerin' frown.

"So ye'd think naught o' stealin' from me, would ye?" he roared. Thanking the eagle fer lookin' oot fer him, the giant carried the lass into his castle, and he said she must be his servant from that day forth. He threw down a bag o' wool before her and told her she must comb it and card it and spin it into yarn before he returned, or else 'twould go hard wi' her.

Then he went away, and the lass wept till she thought her heart would break in two. After a bit she thought she'd better do as the giant said, and she opened the bag o' wool. But there was such a lot o' wool inside that she didna see how she'd ivver manage to comb and card and spin it all before the giant came back. She paced back and forth, and then she spied a pot and a barrel o' meal, and bein' quite hungry after all her weepin', she thought happen she'd have a bit o' porridge to eat before startin' in on the wool.

She hung the pot o'er the fire and made up a nice mess o' porridge. Just as she was sittin' doon to eat it, the door opened and who should come in but a crowd o' the Wee Folk.

"Please might we have a bit o' porridge?" they begged, in their wee shrill voices. But the lass, she was tired and cross and hungry, and she'd not made enough porridge to feed such a crowd.

"I should think not!" she snapped.

When the Cat's Away

"There's little fer one, and less fer two,
And nivver a grain have I fer you!"

With that, the Wee Folk disappeared in
the twinklin' o' an eye. The lass ate her
porridge, and then at last she sat down to
comb and card the wool. But before she
had combed half the wool in the bag, the
giant returned. His three heads roared wi'
rage to see that she'd not finished the task
he set her, and he threw the lass into a
dungeon and said she'd stay there until the
end o' her days.

Now doon in the bonny green glen, the
lass's two sisters sat in their hut worritin'.
When the next mornin' came and the eldest had not returned, the middle sister
said she had best go and look fer her, and
try to get the golden bark. She wrapped
herself in her shawl and set forth up the
mountain.

It went the same fer her as fer her sister.
When she reached the top where the giant
lived, her courage failed her and she sat

weepin' in despair. The eagle swooped
down and asked her what ailed her, and
when she told him, he said happen he'd
fly over the wall and get the bark fer her.
The lass cheered up at once and begged
him to do it, and in a flash he screamed
fer the giant, who took her inside and said
she'd have to be his servant. He left her
wi' the sack o' wool and warned her that
it must all be combed and carded and spun
before he returned, and he left her alone
in her misery.

The lass thought she'd just have a bite
to eat before beginnin', and the moment
she sat doon wi' her porridge, in trooped
the crowd o' Wee Folk again.

"Please, give us a bite to eat!" they
begged, and the lass, feeling as cross and
hungry as her sister had the day before,
waved her spoon at them and told them to
be off.

"There's little fer one, and less fer two,
And nivver a grain have I fer you!"

With that, the Wee Folk disappeared. The lass ate her porridge in peace, and then she set to work on the wool. But the giant returned long before she'd finished, and just as he'd done wi' her sister, he flew into a rage and all his three heads shouted at once, and he tossed the middle sister into the dungeon.

When night had come and gone, and still neither o' her sisters had come doon from the mountain, the youngest lass kenned she must go and look fer them. She laid her shawl upon her mither's bed to warm the poor sick woman, and she kissed her and said she'd soon be home wi' the golden bour-tree bark. Then she tucked a bit o' bread in her apron pocket and set off up the mountain, past the brambles and the common bour-trees, up to the peak where the giant's house lay.

She stood outside the wall, looking at that grim and terrible place, tryin' to summon the courage to knock at the gate. Doon swooped the eagle and asked her what brought her to the giant's house.

"Me mither is ill, and I've come to beg the giant fer a bit o' the bark o' his golden bour-tree," she said. "And also to look fer me sisters, who came here before me and have no returned home."

"Are ye mad, then, child?" cried the eagle. "Do ye truly expect to knock on the giant's door and ask him for help? Why, he'll cut ye into a thousand bits and eat ye in his broth tonight!"

The lass bit her lip, and she said she was afraid o' that very thing. "Indeed, I've a terrible fear that's what has happened to me dear sisters already. I'm that worrited over them, I hardly ken what to do. But me mither lies ill, and I'm her last hope!" She straightened her shoulders and stuck out her determined little chin. "I must bring her that bark, or die tryin'."

The eagle cocked his head and stared at her wi' his bright black eye. "Suppose I were to fly over and get a bit o' the bark fer ye?" he asked. "I could be over the wall and back in the blink o' an eye."

The lass shook her head politely. "Nay, ye'd better not—though 'tis ivver sae kind o' ye to ask. The bark's not mine, and I canna take it wi'oot askin'."

The eagle spread his wings wide and leaped into the sky, wheelin' around above the lass's head.

"Then ye're a wise lass," he called doon, "and I'll give ye a bit o' advice. What's a morsel fer one makes a feast fer another, and what might seem a mountain to ye, others can leap over wi'oot half tryin'."

He flapped away, leavin' the lass starin' after him. She hadna the least idea what he'd meant, but she stored his words away in her mind to think on later.

Then, drawing a deep breath, she knocked on the giant's gate. A great tall door opened up and three ugly heads stared doon at her in surprise.

"Who be ye, and what brings ye to this place?" roared the giant (for bein' a giant, he nivver could speak wi'oot roarin').

The lass introduced herself and explained what she'd come fer. "Sure and I fear me poor mither will die if I dinna bring her back a bit o' the bark from yer golden bour-tree. If ye could spare just a wee bit, I'd be ivver so grateful."

The giant's three heads all stared at her in surprise. 'Twas plain he'd nivver before had someone make so bold as to march right up to his gate and ask him fer a boon—still less a wee snippet o' a lass that he could snap in two like a twig o' kindlin' if he wished. He threw back his heads and roared wi' laughter, and a fearsome grisly sound it was.

"Aye, ye shall have yer bark," he said. "But there's summat ye must do fer me first."

He took her inside and showed her the bag o' wool.

"Ye must comb this and card it and spin it into yarn before sundoon tonight," said the giant. "If ye do it, ye'll have as much golden bark to take home wi' ye as ye like."

"And me sisters?" asked the lass, for she guessed they must be aboot the house somewhere.

Her question set the giant to howlin' and hootin' wi' laughter once mair, and when he'd finished, he said that her sisters might leave wi' her, if she finished the combin' and cardin' and spinnin' before he returned that evenin'. But if she didna finish, he warned her, he'd pitch her into the dungeon wi' the others.

The lass looked at the great huge sack o' wool and wondered how she'd ivver manage to get through it all in a day, but there was naught to be done but to try. She took up the wool comb and began to work. She combed and she combed, and by midday she had combed a great heapin' pile o' wool. But still the sack was bulgin', fer a giant's sack it was, and she had yet the cardin' and spinnin' to do. Her arms were achin' and she was beginnin' to feel weak wi' hunger. She kenned she'd get on faster if she had a bite to eat first, so she took oot the bit o' bread she'd brought wi' her and sat doon to eat it. A meager meal it looked, too, after all her hard work.

Before she took the first bite, the door opened and in came the troop of Wee Folk once more, each o' them nae bigger than a sparrow.

"Please, give us a bite to eat!" they begged, as they had begged her sisters.

The lass looked at all the hungry wee faces, and she looked at the thin slice o' bread in her hand. The eagle's words came back to her—"What's a morsel fer one makes a feast fer another"—and sure it seemed to her that her poor bit o' bread might serve tolerably well to fill such wee bellies.

So she laughed and said,

"There's little fer one, and less fer two,
But there might be a bite fer each o' you!"

She broke the bread into bits and passed them round. And sure enough, the Wee

Folk were so wee indeed that it took no more than a morsel to satisfy each o' them.

When they had finished, they all cried out in thanks. Then, spying the sack o' wool, and the comb, and the cardin' brush, and the spinnin' wheel, they asked the lass in their wee pipin' voices if she'd like their help wi' the work.

The lass looked at the mountain o' wool she had yet to work through, and she doubted such teeny tiny folk would be o' any help at all. But again the eagle's words came to her mind—"What might seem a mountain to ye, others can leap over wi'oot half tryin'."

So she told the Wee Folk she'd be glad o' their help, and in a flurry the tiny creatures set to work. Comb comb comb, card card card, spin spin spin, and as quick as ye'd like, they made their way through the mountain o' wool. They filled bobbin after bobbin wi' the finest, smoothest yarn the lass had ivver seen. She was delighted, and she thanked the Wee Folk gladly. Just as

the sun was sinkin' past the mountain, the Wee Folk filled the last bobbin and off they trooped.

The giant came in, and sure he was amazed to see the bobbins o' yarn all lined up on the floor, and the sack o' wool empty. He scratched his heads one after t'other, and he grumbled a bit, and at last he stomped away and came back wi' the lassie's sisters and also a long strip o' bark he'd peeled from the golden bour-tree. The three sisters, they hugged one another and they wept wi' relief, and then the youngest lass thanked the giant fer his kindness (fer sure and 'twas kind o' him no to have eaten her up in the first place), and they all set off on the path doon the mountain to the bonny green glen. And they made their mither a tea from the bark o' the golden bour-tree, and by the very next mornin' she was as fit as she'd ivver been.

"And noo," said Auld Mary, "we must hie us home to our own bonny glen."

They parted ways at the foot of the Stone House hill, and Martha hurried home. Mum called down to her the moment she entered the house.

"Come upstairs, lass! I've glad news for you!"

Martha raced up to Mum's room. But when she got there, she wished she had gone more slowly. For the glad news turned out to be that Mum had at last found a new governess for Martha, and she was expected to reach Glencaraid in a fortnight.

Miss Lydia Crow

The new governess reached Glencaraid a few days earlier than anyone expected. Martha was down at the shore pitching stones into the water, when she spotted a boat gliding briskly across the loch. At first she thought it was a messenger from Fairlie, for ever since Uncle Harry's family had moved to the valley two years ago, hardly a day had passed that a letter or parcel was not sent across the loch between the Morses and the Drummonds—delicate notes fashionably doused with perfume from Janet for Grisie;

short, neat inquiries from Aunt Grisell, seeking Mum's advice on such matters as the best method of improving a smoking chimney, or how to remove pawprints from one's best upholstered chair; hastily scrawled reports from Uncle Harry to update Father on the progress of his young fir trees; painstakingly neat or smearily blotted notes for Martha from Rachel or Mary, respectively; and even, once, a strange package well wrapped in brown paper, with a series of holes mysteriously punched in the top. This last was addressed to Hedgie, with compliments from cousin Meg. When Martha opened it she had found inside an earthworm, enormously fat, wriggling in a clump of moist soil.

"Miss Meg, she said she didna want yer poor hedger to feel left oot, what wi' all the corryspondence flyin' back and foorth atween Fairlie and here," explained the freckle-faced boy who had delivered the parcel.

Martha had clapped in delight, and with Mum's help she had composed a gracious thank-you note on Hedgie's behalf, to send back to Meg. Mum had poured out some ink into a dish and let Martha dip the hedgehog's paws in it; then they set him loose on a sheet of paper and watched him scrabble about, leaving a trail of funny little black prints. Meg had sent word back that it was the dearest note she had ever received, and she would treasure it all her life.

But this was not the small Fairlie rowboat. This was the ferryboat that people from the village side of the loch could hire to bring them across to the Stone House. It was a large rowboat painted bright green, with two long oars rising and dipping at the sides. Martha could not see who was rowing, though she knew it must be Mr. Shaw, the ferryman, because it was his boat. Mr. Shaw was a very big man, but she could not see him at all— only the oars dipping into the water on each side of the boat. That was because a passenger sat in the bow of the boat in front of him, holding a large gray parasol that blocked his head from Martha's view.

The parasol was held perfectly straight

above the passenger's head. The passenger sat perfectly straight on the low seat of the boat. Martha stared and stared as the boat came closer, but she recognized neither the stiff gray parasol nor the passenger. She had never seen that parasol in kirk. Martha knew every soul who lived in the village, and this lady—it had to be a lady, because of the parasol—was not one of them. She was a stranger.

All at once Martha knew who this person must be. The new governess. She looked at the stiff, straight body and the stiff, straight parasol, and her heart felt squeezed inside her chest. This governess was not fluttery and anxious like Miss Norrie had been. Martha could see that at once from the rigid upright-ness of her posture, although the boat was too far away yet for her to make out the features of the parasol lady's face. The new governess sat utterly still, as if she were made of stone. It made Martha think of the story about her ancestor, Edward MacNab, who was said to have been turned to stone by a water fairy who lived in this very loch. For a moment

Martha wondered if perhaps the new governess had done something to annoy the water fairy as she was getting into the boat, and the fairy had reached up a pale hand and cast a stone spell on the governess without Mr. Shaw even noticing. Or perhaps Mr. Shaw *had* noticed, but he had not known what to do with the stone statue of a strange young lady, and so he was going ahead and bringing her across to the Stone House so that the laird might decide what was to be done.

All this went quickly through Martha's head, but she knew it was only a kind of daydream. No one had ever really seen the water fairy in Loch Caraid, not in Martha's lifetime nor even in her father's. And anyway, a grown-up lady made of solid rock would likely be so heavy she would sink the boat, even a sturdy boat like Mr. Shaw's.

By now the boat had come a little closer, and Martha could see that the passenger was moving after all. Her body remained motionless, but her head was turning slowly to the left and then the right and then back again.

It was clear that she was taking in the view of the shore and the mountains and everything in between. Martha saw her look a long time in the direction of the Creag, and she could not help but wonder if this new governess was already marking it as a place unsuitable for young ladies to visit.

The boat was hastening toward the shore now. Martha stood frozen, staring, forgetting entirely to think about what sort of impression she might be making on the new governess. She almost jumped when she realized the lady was looking right at her. Martha saw piercing eyes, a strong jaw, two smooth wings of brown hair on a broad forehead—and then the boat's bow was nosing into the sand and rocks at the edge of the loch, and Mr. Shaw was drawing in his oars.

The governess waited until the boat had stopped moving, and then she rose to her feet, the parasol rising with her as though it were part of her body. She was dressed all in a dark, somber blue. Her gown was rather old-fashioned, with a low waist and a modest collar. There was not an inch of lace upon her, not even on her bonnet. The bonnet itself was tight and brown and plain, with a narrow brim and a narrow ribbon tied in a no-nonsense bow under the lady's firm chin. Where Miss Norrie had been all ruffles, the new governess was no ruffles at all.

She stepped away from the boat and stood looking at Martha as openly as Martha had been staring at her. Martha could not make out the expression in her dark, probing eyes. The young lady's mouth quirked up at the corners in what might have been amusement or what might have been scorn. It was impossible to tell. The gray parasol cast a shadow over her face. Martha's heart was squeezed so tight it felt like a stone inside her chest. She realized for the first time that she was afraid. She was frightened that the arrival of this straight-backed, parasol-wielding person might mean an end to fun, forever.

This knowledge made her angry. She felt the flash of anger surging through her veins, and that was better than the fear. No stranger

could come to her house and strip away everything that made life pleasant or joyful. Mum would not allow that, no matter how earnestly she wished for Martha to behave like a laird's daughter.

And so without intending to, Martha found herself staring defiantly into the new governess's eyes, with her own spine stretched as straight and tall as she could make it.

The governess spoke up suddenly. "So," she said, "it's not to be love at first sight, is it?"

Martha opened her mouth and closed it without saying anything. She felt her cheeks growing hot. The governess blinked calmly and said, "No matter. The enduring loves seldom are. Look at Shakespeare's Beatrice and Benedict."

Martha had not the faintest idea what the governess was talking about. She watched as the stranger took a small purse out of her pocket and extracted a silver coin, which she put into Mr. Shaw's hand.

"I thank you, sir, for a most pleasant journey," she said, in her precise, clipped voice.

The ferryman mumbled something about carrying her baggage to the house for her, but she held up a hand to prevent him.

"No, thank you, I can manage quite well on my own. But I do appreciate your kindness." She smiled at Mr. Shaw, and Martha was intrigued to see that it was quite a friendly and ordinary smile, such as Nannie might give. This governess was so strange and stiff that Martha had not expected her to be able to smile at all.

"Now then," said the governess briskly, taking hold of the handle of her packing case in one hand and continuing to hold aloft the parasol with the other, "I suppose it's the gray dwelling atop that hill? I was told to look for a stone house."

"*The* Stone House," said Martha, before she knew she was going to speak. The governess looked at her with calm, inquiring eyes. Martha rushed on, feeling she ought to say something. "That's its name."

"I see," said the governess, stepping onto the path that led up the hill. Martha remained a moment at the loch shore beside Mr. Shaw. He glanced sideways at her with a shrug and a crooked grin. She could see that he, too, did not quite know what to make of this odd new-comer. Then, wordlessly, he tipped his cap to Martha and began to ease the ferry backward into the water. Martha found herself running to catch up to the governess.

"And *your* name?" inquired the governess, as if Martha had been beside her all along. "Miss Martha, I presume?"

"Aye," Martha murmured. "Only—I'd rather you didna put in the 'Miss.' "

The governess stopped walking, and she turned to Martha with her mouth quirked up in that same unreadable smile she had smiled at the water's edge. It was not the warm and open smile she had given Mr. Shaw. Martha could not for the life of her tell whether the governess was laughing at her— or whether she was, somehow, pleased by Martha's request.

"I quite understand," said the governess firmly. "We must determine your mother's opinion on that question. My name, incidentally, is Miss Lydia Crow. As I have worn the 'Miss' for thirty-one years, I am quite well accustomed to it. I find it no longer chafes as it once did."

Martha stared goggle-eyed at the strange young lady. Miss Lydia Crow was unlike anyone Martha had ever met. She spoke in riddles; her smile was a riddle; and her right arm, Martha decided, must be the strongest right arm in all of Scotland, able as it was to hold a parasol upright for hours on end without faltering for a second.

House Tour

S omeone in the house must have noticed Miss Crow coming up the path, Martha trailing behind her, for Mollie was waiting to greet them at the front door. She beckoned Miss Crow to go to the parlor. At last the parasol was lowered and folded in on itself. The governess tucked it neatly under her arm. Martha found herself staring at the parasol's point and wondered how much it would hurt if you were pricked with it.

Mum sat on the upholstered chair, her needlepoint on her lap, and smiled up at the newcomer as Miss Crow entered the parlor. Laying the needlepoint aside, she welcomed the governess warmly.

"Do sit down," she said, gesturing toward a chair. "I see you've met my lass."

"I have," Miss Crow answered, nodding crisply. "We made our introductions on the shore. Your loch, by the way, is one of the loveliest I've seen. I spent some time touring the region of Loch Lomond and Loch Katrine. We Lowlanders are quite easily awed by your cliffs and vistas here in the Highlands, you know."

Martha stood uncertainly beside Mum's chair, wondering if she ought to sit down. Mum and Miss Crow were animatedly discussing the relative beauties of Highland and Lowland scenery. Martha had not even known Mum had ever been south to the Lowlands of Scotland. She thought she knew all of Mum's stories; and here was Mum telling new stories to this decorous stranger who seemed more like a weekday caller than a governess reporting for duty.

"Och aye, Ayrshire," Mum was saying. "Is that no where the poet Burns was raised?"

Miss Crow nodded and said it was a privilege to hail from the same county as that remarkable man.

"No poet in history has better captured the spirit and language of our people than Robert Burns," she said with conviction, and softening her voice, she quoted,

> *But pleasures are like poppies spread:*
> *You seize the flow'r, its bloom is shed;*
> *Or like the snow falls in the river,*
> *A moment white—then melts for ever . . .*

"Miss Martha, have you yet heard 'Tam o' Shanter'?" she added, startling Martha, who thought she had been forgotten.

"Nay," Martha murmured, and Mum broke in eagerly, "Is that from his most recent volume? I do hope you've brought a copy, Miss Crow. We've a terrible time getting the latest books and magazines here in Glencaraid."

Martha looked back and forth from Mum

to Miss Crow in wonder. She remembered when Miss Norrie had first arrived at the Stone House. Mum had spent nearly the whole first hour questioning Miss Norrie about her previous engagement and her qualifications. They had discussed mealtimes and bedtimes and lesson times. Certainly no one had quoted poetry.

But then, it did not take much looking to see that Miss Crow and Miss Norrie were as different as different could be.

"Your lass tells me she'd prefer I call her by name only," said Miss Crow suddenly, with an air of getting down to business. "Without the formal title. Have you any objections, madam?"

Mum looked sideways up at Martha, who was still leaning upon the arm of the upholstered chair. "I hope you at least said 'good day' before starting in wi' your list o' likes and dislikes, lass," she teased.

Martha bit her lip, trying to remember if she had. Mum laughed ruefully and said, "Alas! I feared not. Och, Martha, Martha . . ."

Miss Crow said not to worry about it in the slightest, and then she said she would be very grateful for a washbasin in which to rinse the grime of her long journey from her face and hands.

"And after that," she suggested, "perhaps Martha can give me a tour of the house?"

Mum had never answered the question about whether Miss Crow might call Martha simply "Martha," but it seemed to be the kind of question that didn't need an answer. No one ever mentioned it again, and Miss Crow went on leaving off the "Miss." That was the first thing Martha decided she liked about her new governess.

The second thing she liked was that Miss Crow insisted upon seeing every bit of the house, from attic to larder. Miss Norrie had had no interest in rooms other than parlor and nursery, though she had greatly admired Grisie's rosebud bedcurtains. Miss Crow scarcely seemed to notice those bedcurtains, and when she looked around Grisie's room her only comment was, "No books, I see.

Your sister does not care much for reading, Martha?"

"Not very much. Me brother Alisdair does, though. He's read every one of Father's books on the shelf in the parlor," Martha said proudly. "Even the very fattest ones."

"All your brothers are away at school, are they not?"

Martha nodded. She led Miss Crow out of Grisie's room and down the passage toward Mum and Father's bedroom.

"This is where we eat, unless there's company. *Other* company, not living-in company like you," Martha explained. "Och, and there's Grisie!"

Grisie rose from the writing table, where she had been penning another note to Janet. She greeted Miss Crow prettily, and the governess said she hoped Grisie didn't mind that Martha had shown her Grisie's room.

"As long as she didna track anything on my clean floor," Grisie answered Miss Crow. "Martha's a great one for running about wi' dirty feet."

"Grisie!" Martha cried, infuriated. Miss Crow was certain to find out all her faults soon enough; she didn't need Grisie to come right out and say them.

Martha watched Miss Crow's face anxiously to see if she was shocked, but no trace of alarm or dismay appeared in the calm, wide-set eyes. Miss Crow went to the front windows and looked out upon the loch.

"One could almost live on the view here," she said in a tone of satisfaction. "I wonder you can concentrate on your dinners, with all this grandeur just beyond the sill."

"Och, the view's ten times nicer from the terrace at Fairlie," said Grisie. "That's one of my Father's other houses, you know. Our uncle leases it from him. I expect you'll see it next month; my cousins are giving a party."

Miss Crow responded politely and then asked Martha if they hadn't better resume the tour. Martha took her up to the attic and showed her the curtain behind which were Mollie's bed, chest, and washstand. She showed Miss Crow the baskets where the uncarded fleeces and bundles of combed flax were kept, awaiting spinning. She explained how Mollie had to take the fleeces out every now and then, and shake them, and tuck fresh pine branches among them, to make sure the moths weren't getting at the wool. The blazing crimson fleeces that Martha had helped to dye were on top of the basket, all dry now, as richly red as ripe berries. Miss Crow stroked them and said she'd not seen their like before.

"The weavers in Glasgow would pay a small fortune for wool that keeps its color so well," she said. "I ought to know, for my father's a weaver."

"Is he?" Martha exclaimed. "Our Nannie— she was our kitchenmaid, but she got married this summer and left us—her husband Gerry's a weaver, too! I do wish I could see his loom. Me brother Duncan says it's so big it wouldna fit in this room. Are they truly so large?"

Miss Crow chuckled. "Well, you'd have a terrible time of it getting one up the stairs, that's certain. I suppose you could take one apart and rebuild it up here with the loom's castle right underneath the highest part of the roof. That's the part that stands upright in the center of the loom, you know, and holds the harnesses."

"I wish ladies could be weavers," said Martha. "I'd like to try it. Duncan says it makes a great bumping and thumping."

"That it does," said Miss Crow, nodding firmly. "You know, I've a brother who lives in America. He wrote me that over in New England, weaving *is* women's work. He's visited a great many households in which the loom is kept right in the parlor, and after she spins enough yarn to clothe the family, a wife must dye it, weave it, and sew it all on her own. Unless she's so fortunate as to have willing daughters to lend her a hand."

"America!" Martha breathed. This was perhaps the most exciting thing she had ever heard. Miss Crow, who was going to live in this very house, had a brother in America who wrote her letters.

"Will his letters come here, now you're living with us?" she asked.

"My brother's? Aye, I suppose so. And now—I've not yet seen the kitchen."

Martha led Miss Crow eagerly down the attic stairs and then the stone steps to the first floor. Miss Norrie would never have asked to see the kitchen. She had hardly exchanged a dozen words with Cook during the whole half year she had lived in the Stone House, and she had wrinkled her nose in horror when Martha showed her Hedgie in his box and asked if she would like to hold him.

Miss Crow, on the other hand, *asked* to pick up the hedgehog before Martha even had a chance to offer. The lady who had sat so rigidly upright in the boat and on the parlor chair crouched right down beside Hedgie's basket and slipped her hand beneath the plump, spiny little body snuggled in the hay. Gently Miss Crow lifted the hedgehog close to her face, and she looked intently at his pointed brown nose.

Hedgie opened sleepy black eyes and blinked at Miss Crow, and then, as if he were too tired to care that the person holding him was a stranger, he closed his eyes again and settled himself on Miss Crow's hand with a tiny sigh. He did not even bother to raise his spines. Martha heard a humphing noise from the larder doorway behind her, and she turned to see Cook leaning on the doorpost with a bowl of fresh butter in her hands and her eyebrows upraised.

"The lazy beggar," she said curtly, but Martha could see Cook was not at all displeased. Cook pretended not to like Hedgie, but Martha knew she secretly fussed over him like a baby.

"He's charming," whispered Miss Crow, and gently she laid the hedgehog back down in his sweet-smelling nest. "Thank you, Martha, for introducing me."

She stood up and turned to face Cook.

"You must be Miss Margery Anne," she said sociably. "I've been hearing rumors about your fine cooking since before I crossed Loch Caraid."

Cook actually blushed. Martha was choking with laughter.

"Miss Margery Anne, indeed," snorted Cook, shaking her head. "I'm amazed there's a soul in the village still remembers I have a name. Ye can call me Cook, same as the rest o' them. I suppose ye're this Miss Crow I've been hearin' sae muckle aboot?"

"Lydia," said Miss Crow firmly, and Cook broke into a smile.

"Well, ye've a sight mair sense than that Norrie creature, and that's plain," she said. "Happen our Martha will no run ye off quite sae soon. Ye'll pardon me, now; I've just finished the churnin' and I've got to get me butter salted and packed away. This is likely the last churnin' o' butter we'll get this year. The weather's bound to turn soon and the cows'll aye stop givin'."

She disappeared into the main part of the kitchen, humming her churning song under her breath. Miss Crow said Martha must show her the dairy. After she had admired the stoutness of the stone walls that kept it so cool inside, so the milk and butter and cream would stay fresh, she asked for a tour of the garden.

They walked up and down the rows, and Miss Crow seemed interested in every leaf and stalk.

"Your own currant bushes, how splendid! I suppose Cook makes currant cakes now and then?"

"Och, all the time!" Martha said. "Whenever I ask her. They're me favorite."

"Mine, too," smiled Miss Crow. She did not remind Martha to say "my favorite" instead of "me."

That was the third thing Martha liked about the new governess.

More Copywork

At breakfast time the next morning, Miss Crow opened the nursery shutters wide and stuck her head out the window to breathe in the cool draughts of air that rolled down from the mountains.

"Gracious, that's lovely," she announced. "Do you realize how very fortunate you are to live here, Martha? In the city, the air is stale and smoky. There are streets in Glasgow which have not known a breeze in a hundred years."

"I'd nivver want to live in a city," said

Martha decidedly, drying her face at the wash-basin. "I might like to see one, sometime. But only to visit. Grisie wanted to go away to school in Edinburgh, and she was very cross when Father wouldna let her go, but I couldna see why she wanted to. Go and live far away in a house that's all squished in with a row o' other houses? I'd nivver."

"Never is a long time," remarked Miss Crow. "But I quite understand the sentiment."

She turned away from the window and swept her eyes across the nursery. The breakfast porridge and cream were waiting on the table in the middle of the room, and the door of the box bed stood wide open so that the sheets might air out before Mollie came to make the bed. Miss Crow's gaze lingered upon the bed, and as she took her seat at the nursery table, she gave a little shake of her head.

"I shall have to speak to your mother about that bed. It isn't healthful to sleep in such an enclosed space. One seldom comes across one of these old-fashioned box beds anymore. I suppose this one has been in your family for decades."

"I've always slept in it," said Martha, frowning a little. "Ever since I grew out of me cradle."

She did not like the idea of giving up her dear old bed. When she stayed with her cousins at Fairlie, she hated having to sleep in their big, curtained four-poster bed. The bedcurtains billowed and rustled in the night, and all the creakings and thumpings of a night-time house came whispering right through to her pillow. She always felt exposed, and she could not wait to get home to her own safe bed once more.

Martha felt Miss Crow's piercing eyes upon her, and she knew that the governess had noticed the frown. She had begun to like Miss Crow a great deal, and the fear that had arisen inside her heart yesterday on the shore had faded like mist in the sunshine. She did not want this governess to dislike her. But somehow Martha could not help meeting those piercing eyes with a determined stare of her own.

She heard herself saying, "I like me old bed. I dinna want a new one."

And that's that, she thought. She waited for Miss Crow to scold her for having been impertinent.

"Of course you dinna," Miss Crow replied. "I'm pleased to hear it."

Martha blinked. "You are?"

Miss Crow nodded firmly, picking up the cream jug and pouring a modest helping over her porridge.

"Aye, indeed. It shows you have a loyal heart, and that you are not the sort of person who throws something out simply because it's old and worn, and isn't in keeping with the latest fashion." She stirred her cream into the fragrant, steaming oats. "All the same, an open bed really would be better for your health, Martha. And mine as well. I wouldn't suggest it were it not in your best interests. Now, let us say our grace."

It went on like that all day. Every time Martha thought she had begun to understand her new governess, Miss Crow surprised her. After a while Martha decided that the only thing she could safely expect from Miss Crow was that whatever Miss Crow did, it would be completely unexpected.

Miss Crow did not brush Martha's hair roughly, as Miss Norrie had done. Nor did she brush it gently, like Grisie. She did not brush it at all. She said Martha was quite old enough to brush her own hair, and she left Martha alone to do just that.

Martha discovered it was quite a struggle to coax the brush through her knotted curls, and she began to understand why Miss Norrie had had to pull so hard.

Miss Crow put on the same sturdy blue woolen gown she had worn the day before. She brushed and braided her own hair, which was long and thin and straight. With a few quick, practiced motions she coiled the braid into a neat knot and pinned the knot in place. Then she went to the chest into which she had unpacked her things the day before, and she took out a crisp linen apron. It was very plain, but finely woven.

Martha had wriggled into her own frock, a gray linen everyday dress. She went to Miss

Crow to have her apron tied, but the governess would not do that either.

"You ought to be able to manage it yourself," she said, just as she had said about the hairbrushing. "Just reach your arms around back like this—see? And now you make the bow."

Martha felt a little thrill of victory when she tied the bow and the bow stayed tied. Then she felt foolish, for having asked in the first place. Someone else had always tied her apron and brushed her hair. It had never occurred to her to do those things herself. Miss Crow would think she was a baby.

Because she did not want to be thought a bairn, she didn't ask Miss Crow if she might run in and say good morning to Mum. Miss Norrie had always scolded Martha for doing that; she said Mrs. Morse had enough to attend to and that was what she paid a governess's wages for: to keep Martha out from under her feet. Martha had never been able to hear those words without retorting that Miss Norrie was as wrong as wrong could be. Then Miss Norrie would blink and shake her head and stare as if to say, what can you do with such an impertinent child as this?

Martha had a feeling that Miss Crow would have an altogether different way of responding to impertinence. So she did not ask to go see Mum, though she was aching to do so. A morning couldn't start right without a kiss from her mother.

It turned out that she didn't need to ask. As soon as the nursery had been made neat and tidy, Miss Crow said, "And now I suppose your mother is waiting to see you. Hurry along, and afterward we shall take a nice walk. We must fill up our lungs with some of the fresh air of which they were deprived all night."

Martha all but flew to her mother's room.

"How do you like your new governess, lassie?" Mum asked, after Martha had received her kiss.

"I think I like her very much," answered Martha frankly. "Only she wants to get rid of me bed."

She realized suddenly that the question of the box bed was so far the only thing about Miss Lydia Crow to which she objected. And there were so very many things to like—imagine, a governess who wanted to take a walk outdoors first thing in the morning!—that Martha began to feel the bed was not quite so important after all.

She told Mum what Miss Crow had said about the bed, and Mum pursed her lips thoughtfully and said the matter was worth discussing. Then Miss Crow appeared in the doorway, greeted Mum cheerfully, and asked if Martha was ready for her walk.

A walk with Miss Crow on a Glencaraid morning, the mist still heavy upon the loch and the cool sharp smell of autumn rising under the peat smoke, was a glorious thing. Miss Crow asked the names of every mountain and she asked in particular about the Creag.

"I noticed it from the boat yesterday. I expect you've a fine view of the loch and the mountains from up there," she said, staring into the mist in the direction of the steep, rocky hill. "What lies beyond it?"

"The moor, and Auld Mary!" cried Martha, and she told Miss Crow all about them. By the time they had walked the loch shore path as far as the foot of the Creag, Miss Crow knew nearly as much about Auld Mary as did anyone else in the glen.

"She sounds very wise," said Miss Crow. "'Tis a grand thing, to have a friend like that. Come, I suppose we'd better get back to the house. Duty beckons!"

When it came to lessons, Martha soon discovered that Miss Crow was far more strict than Miss Norrie had been. She did not hover nor flutter, and there was no anxious hand-wringing whatsoever. She told Martha firmly what was expected of her, and then she took out a large and bulky piece of knitting and proceeded to knit with all her might and main. Martha sat at the nursery table with her copy-book and inkwell before her, and she labored harder than she had ever done to make the letters neat and even.

I to the hills will lift mine eyes,
From whence doth come mine aid.

Martha had copied thus far from the hymnal when a flash of movement caught her eye: a wee house mouse, streaking along the base of the wall beneath the nursery window. She often saw mice in the Stone House at this time of year; their nests in the hay meadow had all been destroyed during the mowing, and they could hardly be blamed for seeking shelter elsewhere. If Cook caught a glimpse of one sneaking around her larder, she took after it with a broom, but Martha did not mind seeing the occasional mouse upstairs, so long as it did not run across her covers at night.

This particular mouse scurried the length of the wall and disappeared behind the clothespress. Seeing it called to Martha's mind a poem she had learned the year before, about another mouse whose nest had been destroyed. And that made her think of Robert Burns, the poet. She wondered when she would get to hear the new poem Miss Crow had mentioned—what had she called it? Tam o' Something. Martha screwed up her eyes and tried to remember the lines Miss Crow had quoted.

After a moment she had the feeling that someone was watching her, and she opened her eyes with a start. Miss Crow was still staring intently down at her knitting, so motionless but for her brisk and busy hands that Martha was certain her woolgathering had gone unnoticed. The long wooden needles went *tap tap tap* against each other, and the yarn quivered and looped, and the long-fingered hands bent and swiveled. Beyond that, nothing moved. Miss Crow was a stone lady again, only this time without the parasol.

But still Martha had the feeling that her every move was being watched. As if to confirm this suspicion, Miss Crow, eyes still fixed upon the needles, slowly raised her left eyebrow. Martha jumped as though the governess had pricked her with a pin. She wrenched her gaze back to her copywork and wrote without daring to look up until all the assigned lines had been copied.

Miss Crow seemed to know exactly when Martha was finished, for Martha had just finished the last letter of the last word when the governess laid the knitting aside. She rose and looked at the copywork. Martha waited anxiously for stern words about the blots. Miss Crow was such a precise person; it did not seem likely that she would stand for any sort of untidiness.

But the governess merely nodded her head once and said, "Now then, let us have a look at your sewing."

Martha brought out the sash, which was nearly finished now. She had kept her promise to Mum; she had worked steadily on it and had not complained. But secretly she hated that sash. She had never cared much for it to begin with, and ever since the flax-bundling day, it gave her an ache inside whenever she picked it up. Each time she laid down a new stitch, she thought of the ruined silk thread.

The homespun linen thread Mum had given her in place of the silk did not have the same magical sheen. The few silken flowers she had put into the far end of the sash before using the thread to tie flax shimmered in the light; light seemed to cling like dew to the lustrous red petals and the dazzling golden ones. The petals of the linen-thread flowers were flat and dull.

Mum had asked Martha just yesterday if she thought she might have the sash finished in time for the party at Fairlie. Martha would have to wear that sash in front of her cousins, and most likely someone would tell the story of the flax bundles. Cousin Janet would giggle, and Rachel would stare at Martha in that blank mystified way she had. Rachel never could understand why Martha did the things she did.

But when Miss Crow held the sash and looked at the needlework up and down its length, she did not comment on the unfortunate shift from silk to linen. She said only, running her fingers lightly over a tulip worked in creamy yellow linen, "Gracious, what rich color. I cannot get over the quality of the dyestuffs here. My father would pay a pretty penny for linen this fine. Did your Auld Mary dye this lot as well?"

"I dinna ken," said Martha, taken aback. "It might have been Mollie and Nannie. That yellow comes from naught but buckthorn. It's nothing so bright as the gold Auld Mary can get from heather. She showed me just how to do it, too."

She felt proud, being able to talk so knowledgeably about dyes and dyestuffs to the daughter of a big-city weaver—prouder still that Miss Crow was so impressed with the thread that had been grown and harvested and spun and colored, every bit, by her own friends. The flax had grown on Father's land a year ago, and Mrs. Sandy and the Tervishes and the Shaws and Lew and Ian and the others had pulled it, and Mum herself had spun it, or Grisie. Then the dyeing, and now the sewing—she saw suddenly that her hands were the last in a chain that linked nearly every soul in Glencaraid to one another. All of them, together, had worked to create that sash. It was not just Martha's sash; it belonged to all of them, and she found that she hated it no longer.

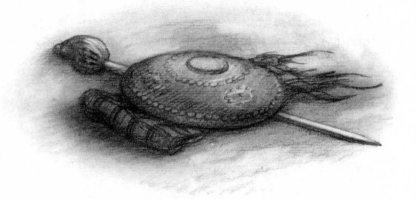

Culloden and the Crofter

It surprised Martha to see how quickly the days passed now that Miss Crow had come. Days with Miss Norrie had been slower than a two-legged sheep, as Cook would say. Miss Crow kept things snapping along. She asked Martha how many poems she could recite, and when Martha said none, Miss Crow raised her hands in mock horror.

"We'll have to remedy that!" she said, and she set Martha a stanza of "Tam o' Shanter" to memorize from a book she had brought in her trunk. At first Martha groaned inside, for this seemed like another kind of copywork. But after Miss Crow had read her the whole poem through once, Martha was hungry to learn it. It was a tale, a creepy, chilling kind of tale that was every bit as good as one of the yarns Cook liked to spin as she stirred her broth beside the fire on gloomy winter afternoons. Tam was a foolish man who wandered into great danger one stormy night when:

The wind blew as 'twas blawn its last;
The rattling showeres rose on the blast;
The speedy gleams the darkness swallow'd;
Loud, deep, and lang the thunder
bellow'd—

When Miss Crow read those words, her voice crooned like the wind. The hair prickled on the back of Martha's neck, and her heart thumped. It nearly stopped altogether when the unfortunate Tam rode his faithful horse right into a party of witches dancing a foul and evil dance in the howling woods. Martha ran to Miss Crow's side and, all unawares, clutched the governess's arm while Tam quailed with fear atop his good horse, Maggie, who ran like the wind with the pack of witches close on her tail.

Afterward Martha felt surprised to see the sunbeams slanting through the nursery windows, painting the floor with gold. Part of her was still in the midnight woods with Tam and Maggie. Miss Crow gave her the book, and Martha learned two whole stanzas before dinner that day.

Autumn raced past like Tam o' Shanter's horse. October went out in a blaze of light, for a bonfire burned on every hilltop on All Hallows' Eve. Then came All Saints' Day, with its candles and singing. After supper that night, Mum told the story she told every year on All Saints', about how her mother had entrusted her children to the care of St. Michael after the bloody Battle of Culloden in 1746. Mum's own father had died in that battle, while she was still a babe in her mother's womb.

"'Twas well known my father was a Jacobite, and loyal to the line of King James.

Sure and all the Drummonds were. When James's fine son, our dear bonny prince, sailed from France to gather an army that might rescue the throne of Scotland from the usurper King George, my father was among the first in line to join up. Bonny Prince Charlie and his brave men made a stalwart fight of it, they did. I'll warrant there was many a man among the English army whose knees quaked in terror at the sight and the sound of the prince and his lads with their shields flashing and their swords waving, and the calm fierce fire in their eyes.

"But that George, he had all the armies in England at his disposal—and a good many Lowland Scots, too. And I mean no offense to you, Miss Crow, for I suppose your own grand-father was likely among them. We're none of us to blame for the politics o' our fathers."

"No offense taken," said Miss Crow placidly, her knitting needles clicking in their steady rhythmic way. Martha thought she might say more, but she merely smiled and went on knitting.

"But I want to ken!" Martha couldn't help bursting out. "*Was* he? Your grandfather? Did he fight for King George?"

"Hush, Martha, your mother's in the midst of a tale," scolded the governess gently.

And Father said sternly, "Martha, you leave Miss Crow be."

So Martha closed her mouth and sat meek as a moorhen on her stool beside the hearth. But inside she was burning to know if Miss Crow's grandfather had fought at Culloden. Why . . . perhaps he had been the very man who slew her own grandfather!

That thought gave her a queer feeling inside, so that she was glad to stop thinking and go back to listening to Mum instead.

"Aye, King George had more men and more money. His troops were better fed and better armed than the army of the Young Chevalier. So it was that in April of 1746, Prince Charlie's army fell at the hands of the English troops. My own father, so they say, took out ten Englishmen before he was mown down by a cavalry soldier. Few Highlanders survived to tell the tale of that grim battle. And Bonny Prince Charlie escaped by the skin o' his teeth, with a price on his head. He made his way at great peril over the mountains and across the moors to the coast, where at last he boarded a ship and returned, broken-hearted, to France. And that was the end o' the second Jacobite rising o' forty-five.

"After the battle, King George ordered his men to punish the clans who had stood up for the Stuart prince. My mother heard the news from a Jacobite soldier who'd managed to escape from the king's men. This man rode like the wind to warn the families of all the killed or captured lairds that English troops were coming their way. He had to tell my mother that my father was dead, and the sorrow nearly killed her. But she had no time to grieve. The king's men were coming.

"In great haste my mother threw a few precious things into a sack and snatched up my brother Harry, who was a tiny wee thing just two years old. The servants helped her onto a horse—and her a woman heavy with child, for I was due to be born within the month! And crying out to the saints and angels to protect her, she rode fast as lightning into the hills.

"A terrible time she had of it, that night, and the next, and the next. Every minute she lived in terror that a party o' English soldiers would come upon her, and slay her wee son, and put her on a boat headed for the Americas. And she thought o' her lovely house that she'd left behind, and wondered if ever she'd see it again.

"Sure and no one could, for the king's army burned it to the ground a day after she left. My father's lands were taken by the English, and another man holds their title today."

Martha shivered, and she scooted her stool closer to Grisie. Grisie reached down and took one of Martha's hands in her own. Father was staring into the darkness, his eyes shadowed. Even Miss Crow had fallen idle, her needles held motionless in mid-loop.

Mum's voice was soft and low. "After the third day o' hard riding—she was headed for the coast, for she thought she might find passage to the Isle of Skye, where she had some kin—my mother felt what she'd dreaded most. Her labor was beginning; and the pain was fearsome. My birthing time had come too soon.

"She was miles from anywhere, all alone in the hills wi' no one but the red deer and the wild grouse to hear her moans. She half fell off her horse and begged him to stay close, for there was neither tree nor post to tie him to. Harry was crying, as well he might, the poor hungry wee lad. She wrapped him in a plaid and pinned it beneath a stone so that he might not wander off and come to harm, and she gave him her last crust o' bread to eat.

"And her pains came on, faster and faster, and sure she kenned I was coming.

"She dared not cry out for help—for still she feared the enemy soldiers. She bit her lips to keep from screaming out in her pain, until the blood flowed down from her beautiful mouth. And at last the pain was so great she could bear it no more, and she thought surely she would die. She cried out to St. Michael the Archangel to take care o' her son, and her babe, too, if by some miracle it lived.

"By now my brother had finished his crust o' bread, and he had set his wee mind to freeing himself from that stone. Never a lad to allow for the passin' o' a single moment in peace, your Uncle Harry."

Mum smiled a little and shook her head. Martha nearly flew off her stool in her agony to hear what came next.

"Go on, go on!" she cried.

Mum laughed at her and nodded. "Aye, and there's a sight more to tell. That rascal Harry, he wriggled his way out o' the plaid altogether, he did. And while my mother huddled against the side o' her horse in anguish, Harry left his blanket lying there with the great heavy stone still pinning it to the ground. He wandered off a little way around the curve of the hill. And there he found a stream that ran between the hills and watered a small croft some little way off.

"I suppose wee Harry must have been

thirsty, after gulping down his dry bread. Whatever the case, he went boldly forward toward the bright water, and sure as day his foot slipped on the muddy bank. With a great splash and a plop, he fell right into the water.

"My mother heard the splash and thought it was a soldier's horse crossing a stream to get her. She had no notion, o' course, that her small son had gone a-roaming—her eyes were that blinded with tears and sweat and fright.

"Someone else heard the splash, too. 'Twas the very crofter whose farm lay downstream. Now this fellow, he was a young man who lived alone with his auld parents, for he'd not yet found himself a wife. His father was blind, and his mither was poorly, and the lad had a heavy burden to bear, keeping the farm running and the rent paid and food on the table for the three o' them. And as if that weren't enough, he'd fallen from the house roof some weeks earlier, while he was fixing a hole in the thatch, and he'd hurt his back something terrible. Not a step had he taken since, that wasna shot through with a fiery pain. He'd struggled through the pain to keep the stock fed, but he couldna manage any work beyond that. There was no denying that if he didna get better soon the farm was bound to fail. It was a hard fate to fall upon such a good hard-working lad.

"Well, that very morning he'd awakened to discover that by some miracle, the pain was gone. He stretched in his bed, and he marveled at how fit and strong he felt.

"'Mither!' he cried. 'Me back has mended. I'm as hale as ivver I was, if ye can believe it!'

"Och, how relieved his poor mither was, and how glad his auld ailing father. The lad wanted to run out and see to the plowing and the shoveling and the chopping right away, for the farm was in a sorry state after his weeks of illness. But his mither, she feared he'd over-tax himself the first day out o' bed, and she begged her son to spend at least one day at his leisure, taking a nice long walk to stretch out his muscles.

"Reluctantly the lad obeyed, and that's how

he came to be strolling along beside the stream in a place he'd never have been on an ordinary day, just when my naughty brother went plunging headlong into the water.

"The young crofter was that surprised to see a wee boy bobbing in the stream, he hardly kenned what to think. He'd not seen where the bairn came from, and for all he kenned, Harry had fallen straight down from heaven! But he gathered his wits quickly and splashed out into the water, and saved the little rogue from drowning.

"'Whence came ye, me lad?' he asked Harry, and he turned this way and that to see who the child might belong to. And he heard a nicker, and then a low crying moan, coming from just over the crest o' the hill.

"With Harry dripping water all over his clothes, the crofter hurried around the hill, and there he found my mother, her face deadly white with pain and fear. He saw at a glance what was happening, and he ran to my mother's side. He asked if she had time for him to fetch his mither, for the auld woman was a fine midwife who'd brought many a bairn through a difficult birth. My mother told him to take her horse, and be quick about it.

"And so it was that not a quarter of an hour later a skilled midwife was kneeling beside my mother and calming her with gentle words, and a little while after that I came screaming and kicking into the world. The crofter got my mother home, and his mither saw her settled safely in bed with me lying beside her, nursing for all I was worth, and they dried off my brother and gave him a bowl o' porridge to quiet his howls and his hunger.

"My mother stayed three months with the family, for she was too ill to move. They kept the secret of her presence, for King George's soldiers were still roaming the hills seeking to punish the families of the bonny prince's loyal soldiers. My mother, she entrusted the crofter with the little bit of gold and jewels she'd managed to bring away with her, and she begged him to promise that if anything happened to her, he would see that her children were delivered to her aunt and uncle in Skye. She offered him her horse as a reward, but he refused to take it.

"'Ye'll be well enough yet to ride him yerself,' protested the young man. But in this he was mistaken. My mother died at the end of three months' time, and the crofter, he kept his promise. He took Harry and me to Skye, and we grew up there far from the Drummond lands and the house of our father that was no more."

Mum was quiet, staring into the fire. After a long time, Miss Crow's needles began to click again.

"Was it really all St. Michael's doing?" asked Martha breathlessly.

"Who can say?" Mum mused. "We've no way to ken for sure. But one thing is certain. That young crofter's back had kept him in bed for three weeks, and it's a strange thing indeed that the pain left him so suddenly the very morning my mother needed his aid.

"And another thing. That lonely croft was the only dwelling place for many a long mile around. The landowner in those parts was a supporter of King George, who'd have been glad to turn my mother over to the English in hopes of a fat reward. Most of his tenants would have done the same thing. But the young crofter and his family were Jacobites at heart, and better than that, they were honest to the bone. Your Uncle Harry couldn't have chosen a better spot to go tumbling into the water, nor a safer moment.

"The crofter told my great-aunt that my poor mother had wanted to christen me Michael—but when she heard I was a lass, she changed it to Margaret, after the crofter's auld mither who delivered me."

Dance at Fairlie

By the day of the party at Fairlie, Martha had learned all of "Tam o' Shanter" by heart. She stood before the nursery fire and recited the whole ballad for Miss Crow. The governess was pleased. She said Martha had a fine flair for elocution.

"Perhaps you can recite for the guests at your uncle's party," Miss Crow suggested.

Martha wrinkled her nose. She wasn't sure how she felt about that idea. Miss Crow would not be there to help her if she got stuck; Mum had said the governess might have the day off while the family was across the loch at Fairlie.

"I wish you were coming to the party," she said wistfully. "It'll be almost as much fun as Nannie's wedding feast. Uncle Harry has a lot of dogs, and they howl when people sing."

Miss Crow laughed. "It does sound lively. But methinks your uncle's house will be full enough without me. Your mother says a good many of the guests will stay overnight, and your Aunt Grisell is in a tither as to where to put them all."

"Whisht! There's hundreds o' beds at Fairlie!" scoffed Martha. Miss Crow lifted an eyebrow, and Martha shrugged. "Dozens, at least. And they're all the kind o' bed you'd approve of—four-poster beds like Grisie's. With curtains that rustle and shiver all night long."

She shuddered. Her nights in her own dear box bed were numbered, Martha knew. Mum and Father had agreed with Miss Crow that it was time Martha's old-fashioned bed was retired.

Miss Crow smiled at her.

"I asked your mother if your old bed could perhaps be stored in one of the barns, where you could go and play in it from time to time. 'Twill make a fine wee playhouse, don't you think?"

Martha drew in her breath in delight, for she saw at once the rich possibilities for play such a house would provide.

"Aye, if we took out the mattress, the house would have a real wood floor—and I could have a stool to sit on—and I can make a little ring o' stones for a fireplace in the middle, like in Annie's cottage. Cook'll give me a peat to pretend I've a fire with, I ken it! And the barn cats can live with me there, like Auld Mary's cat. . . ."

Miss Crow moved about the nursery, tidying up. She had the kind of busy hands that never stopped moving; they were always tidying or knitting or sewing or turning the pages of a book. But all the while, Martha could see that Miss Crow was listening, really listening, like Mum listened when Martha spoke. Miss Norrie had never seemed interested in the things Martha had to say.

Martha remembered the horrible moment of fear she had felt when Miss Crow first stepped out of the ferryman's boat upon the shore of Glencaraid. The memory nearly made her laugh now, it was so silly to think of worrying about Miss Crow's arrival. Miss Crow was like Cook and Auld Mary: she was someone you wanted to keep around you forever.

"Come," said Miss Crow briskly, putting her book of poems back into its place on the little writing table Father had given her. "Take out your sash. You must finish that last flower cluster this morning, so that you may wear it at the party."

The morning passed quickly while Martha labored over the last embroidered petals on the sash. Then it was dinnertime, and after that Mum made her lie down for a while, so that she would be rested for the party that evening. Martha lay on the box bed in her long-sleeved woolen shift, trying obediently to sleep and failing miserably, as she had known she would. She didn't see how anyone could be expected to fall asleep right in the middle of the day, especially a day with great excitement waiting just beyond the chime of the clock. The bed felt hot and stuffy—because it was day, she supposed, and the fire was burning brightly just beyond the bed's wooden door panel. She opened the door to let a little air in. Then she snatched her arm back into the bed for fear someone would come in to check on her just at that moment, and catch her playing.

Try to sleep, Mum had said, and so she tried. But she kept forgetting to close her eyes, and then she would remember and squeeze them shut again. She could hear footsteps below her in the kitchen. Miss Crow was down there, visiting with Mollie and Cook. Martha was half mad with curiosity to know what they were talking about down there.

After a long, long time, she heard footsteps coming up the stairs and down the hall, closer, closer, and then a hand rattled the knob of the nursery door. Martha stuck her head out the box bed doorway to see who it was.

"You may get up now," said Miss Crow's voice. There was laughter in it. "I needn't say 'wake up,' need I? Cook said there was more chance of a whale surfacing in Loch Caraid than of your getting a nap today. Come, you must get dressed for the party."

After the long, dull hour in bed, it was lovely to have to scurry around getting ready. Martha wriggled her way into the new woolen cold-weather dress Mum had made her. It was a rich earth-brown color, with cream-colored lace for trim. The lace was the same color as the embroidered sash, and the red and yellow flowers on the sash matched the ribbons Miss Crow tied into Martha's hair: one small bow on top of her head and a large one at the nape of her neck. Martha could feel the edges of the large bow tickling her ears when she turned her head. She craned her neck down to look at the sash. From that angle the embroidered flowers looked quite respectable.

Through the nursery walls came the sounds of Grisie and Mum and Father all hurrying to put on their own party clothes. Martha heard

Father grumbling that his wig would not sit properly unless Mum fixed it; and Mum said she would see to it as soon as Mollie had finished dressing her hair, and for goodness' sake not to get himself in a frenzy about it. Grisie shrieked down the hall that she could not find her black kid slippers, and Mollie called back that she had polished them this morning and they were sitting on the hearth in Grisie's room, and Grisie called back that oh, yes, there they were, right in front of her. Martha and Miss Crow looked at each other and burst into laughter. Martha wondered if the party itself could be as much fun as this.

Father had sent for the ferry, and as soon as everyone was dressed and brushed and made as splendid as could be, they bundled into warm wraps and hurried down the path to the shore. Mr. Shaw was waiting. He had spread rugs upon the boat's board seats for the Morses to sit on, for it was cold upon the water. Martha waved at the Stone House in case Miss Crow was watching out the parlor window. She wished again that Miss Crow were coming to the party. The governess had not yet seen Fairlie, the grand and beautiful house. It was not nearly so cozy and homey as the Stone House, but Martha thought it was certainly a sight worth seeing.

Uncle Harry had sent his carriage to meet them at the lake shore. His beautiful brown horses stood waiting, shaking their glossy heads and puffing with their nostrils. Martha longed to ride one, but she was hustled into the carriage right away and hustled back out again only a few moments later. They had arrived at Fairlie, where candles shone like stars in the windows.

"Mercy! Grisell must be burning a month's worth of candles tonight," Mum murmured.

"It's lovely," breathed Grisie, her eyes shining like the candles. She loved the beauty and splendor of Uncle Harry's house.

A servant ushered the family into the grand Fairlie ballroom, which glowed with the light of so many candles and oil lamps that it was like an All Hallows' hilltop. The large, open room was already crowded with guests. Martha's eyes were dazzled by the bright silk gowns and the vibrant tartan kilts and jackets. A trio of fiddlers in red breeches stood beside the pianoforte, playing with vigor. Martha saw that Lew Tucker's brother was one of them, and the village schoolmaster sat at the pianoforte, his long-fingered hands flying over the keys.

The cousins came hurrying over to greet Martha and Grisie, and guests crowded around Father and Mum, bowing to them and wishing them well. Uncle Harry lived in the grand house, but really it belonged to Father. Watching them, Father in his crimson coat and Mum in her shimmering wine-colored silk, Martha felt bursting with pride and yet curiously small at the same time. There were so many people, and they were all so fancy and fine. She didn't know many of them. At Nannie's wedding Martha had known every soul present. She had sat in kirk with them, raced their children on the moor, eaten bannocks in their cottages. Here, in a house that belonged to her own father and was lived in by her own uncle, she felt like a stranger.

Still, it was fun to watch the dancing, and
to move in and out among the guests with
Mary and Rachel, discussing the gowns and
the hairstyles. Aunt Grisell had invited guests
from all over the county—so many guests that
Uncle Harry's stables could not hold all the
horses. His treasured carriage could not be put
back in the carriage house, for some of the
horses had had to be stabled there. All through
the long evening of dancing and laughter,
Uncle Harry kept going to the window to make
sure it hadn't begun to rain. He loved his carriage next after his wife, his children, and his
dogs—Mum teased that he'd choose that carriage over her, his only sister, if it came down
to a choosing.

"The de'il take me if I did," protested
Uncle Harry in his hearty, booming way. "A
man can buy another carriage, if he should
chance to lose the first. But a sister sae bonny
as me Margaret canna be fetched for any price!
Come, then, Meggie, let's show these heavy-
footed slowpokes how to cut a reel," and he
took Mum's hands and whirled her out into

the throng of dancing couples.

Mum and Uncle Harry seldom acted like grown-ups when they were together. Mum said Uncle Harry never could see her as anything but the little sister who had plagued his steps all over their auntie's rambling old house on the Isle of Skye.

Grisie, on the other hand, seemed more grown-up than ever. All the past year she had been growing so gentle and fine that Martha kept wondering where her old sister had gone. It was like one of Cook's fairy changeling stories—someone had crept in and taken the old Grisie, and left in her place this tall young woman with the glossy curls quivering on her neck and the mysterious glimmer in her eye.

Aunt Grisell's guests begged Grisie and the young-lady cousins to sing. Blushing, Grisie and Janet let themselves be led to the pianoforte in front of the assembled party. Grisie played for cousin Janet, and Grisie's playing was a great deal better than Janet's singing.

Then Janet played, and Grisie sang, and Martha saw how some of the young men held their breath so as not to miss a note of her clear, sweet, lovely song.

After that Martha watched those young men very closely. She did not quite like the way they hovered around her pretty sister, nor how shiningly they smiled when Grisie consented to a dance.

During one dance, cousin Meg saw how Martha was watching and came to stand beside her.

"Like moths to a flame, aren't they?" she murmured cheerfully. "Our Grisie is the beauty of the county."

"She is?" asked Martha. She felt herself frowning a little. She was proud to have such a beautiful sister, but there was something unsettling about all this attention Grisie was getting from the young men in their powdered wigs and brushed jackets.

A sudden thought came into her mind, and she said to Meg, "Grisie and Nannie are nearly the same age, and Nannie's a married lady."

"Aye," said Meg, who was a year younger than Grisie. "That's true. But I'd not start worrying about the wedding clothes yet, Martha. Janet's the one who's pining for a husband, not your Grisie. Grisie's a sensible lass, and she'll wait for the right man."

Martha stared at Meg with narrowed eyes. Now it was Meg talking like a grown-up—jolly cousin Meg, who still wore her hair long and loose, and who, a week ago, was said to have been seen eating jam out of a jar in the larder!

"My gracious, Martha!" laughed Meg, her round face crinkled with amusement. "You look as if we're talking of funerals, not weddings!"

Just then the dance ended, and Aunt Grisell came rustling over and said it was time for little girls to be in bed.

"Miss Caldwell will help you get settled," she said, and the cousins' governess took a candle and ushered Rachel, Mary, and Martha up the winding stair. Martha wondered what Miss Crow was doing at home on her night off. Reading, most likely. Miss Crow was always reading, unless she was knitting.

Miss Caldwell, the cousins' governess, hung up the party dresses while the girls put on their nightgowns, and then she pushed aside the bedcurtains and stood beside the bed to hear their prayers.

After all the food and the music and the noise, Martha was so tired that for once the billowing and whispering of the cousins' bed-curtains did not trouble her a bit. She snuggled in with Mary on one side and Rachel on the other, and she fell asleep thinking of Grisie shining like a candle, with the young men hovering like moths to be near her.

Next Morning

S he awoke to a brisk noise of footsteps. Someone hurried past the nursery, and then another someone followed, and there were voices downstairs and a sudden uproar of dogs barking. Martha and Rachel and Mary sat up in bed and looked at each other.

"Is it still the party?" Mary asked, blinking sleep out of her eyes.

"Not with the dogs," said Rachel. "Mother would never let them in the house around ladies in ball gowns."

"Anyhow, it's morning," said Martha. Stripes of sunlight angling through the shutters made a pattern of lines on the rosy bedcurtains. The girls sat still a moment, listening to the agitated voices and the sound of doors opening and closing. Uncle Harry's dogs went galloping down a hallway, their claws clacking on the floorboards. Then there was a stern roar from Uncle Harry, and the clacking abruptly ceased.

"Something has happened," said Rachel, and suddenly all three of them were scrambling out of bed at once. Rachel stood uncertainly in the middle of the nursery for a moment, looking back and forth between the clothespress and the door, but Martha gave no thought to getting dressed. She wrenched open the door, hurried out into the passageway, and ran barefoot to the landing to look down on the main hall below.

Father and Uncle Harry were just going out the wide front doors, followed by the mob of Uncle Harry's dogs. The men were fully dressed and they carried their guns. Mum and

Aunt Grisell, wearing linen wrappers over their nightdresses, were standing in the hall, watching them go. Uncle Harry's steward came out of a downstairs room and hurried outside behind the dogs, and in the upstairs rooms doors were opening and bleary-eyed party guests were poking their heads into the hall.

"We'd better get dressed," said Mum, and she turned toward the stairs just as Martha was coming down. Mary was right behind her and Rachel waited anxiously in the nursery doorway.

"Och, you're awake, are you, lasses?" said Mum. "It's early yet."

Martha ran down the stairs and clutched at Mum's bed wrapper. "What's happening? Where are they going?"

"Hush, child, you need not worry," Mum soothed. "A dreadful thing has happened to your uncle's trees, but there's no danger. Except to the trees," she added, her forehead creasing angrily. "Those fools!"

"What fools?" Martha asked.

217

Mum didn't answer, and Aunt Grisell chimed in.

"Never you mind. It's naught you need concern yourself with, child. Go on back to the nursery and play quietly like the good lasses you are. Och, Mrs. Biggins! Did the noise wake you? I'm so terribly sorry."

Reluctantly the girls turned and trudged back up the stairs. Mrs. Biggins, one of the party guests, had come to the top of the landing. She eyed Martha and Mary accusingly as they passed, as if all the noise and commotion had been their fault. Her eyes were red and sleepy, and her tight nightcap gave her the look of a newly shorn sheep. Last night she had had great heaps and swirls of hair piled atop her head; but that hair sat upon a wigstand now. Mary's eyes went wide at the sight of her, as if she feared Mrs. Biggins would gobble her up. Martha grabbed her hand and pulled her back to the nursery, where Rachel hurriedly shut the door behind them.

It was maddening, not knowing what was going on. Martha could not imagine what might have happened to Uncle Harry's trees. She supposed Mum had been talking about the young firs Father had encouraged Uncle Harry to plant last year. Father had had great success with his own tree plantations; the new trees helped to shield the food crops from the fierce winds that swept down from the mountains. Uncle Harry, taking Father's advice, had put in a long, wide border of trees along the margins of his oat and barley fields. Martha had been taken to see them: the dainty little trees in their tidy rows like an army of elves in green coats.

She wondered if there could possibly have been a storm last night, during the wee hours when she was deep asleep. It didn't seem likely. A storm wild enough to harm the trees would surely have been too loud to sleep through. And anyway, Mum could not have been talking about wind nor rain when she said, "Those fools."

The girls hurried into their clothes and waited for Helen, the upstairs maid, to bring their breakfast. Miss Caldwell came in to see that their hands and faces were properly washed. She would not tell them anything about the trees.

"Don't worry yourselves about what doesn't concern you," she said. "Now stay here and for mercy's sake, be quiet. The house is full of people and half of them will expect to sleep until noon. I must go see to Baby."

She bustled off to get Eamonn dressed and fed. Martha thought if one more person told her to be quiet, she would scream.

When Helen came with the breakfast tray, Martha and Mary fairly pounced on her.

"Whisht! Ye'll upset the cream!" Helen fussed, her arms swaying to keep the tray in balance. "Hungry, are ye, Miss Rachel?"— for Rachel was sitting quietly at the nursery table with her hands folded before her. Martha saw how the frown creased Rachel's forehead. She had been sitting there not because she was hungry, but to show what a good girl she was. But Martha could not stop to worry about Rachel.

"We want to know what happened!" she demanded.

"Aye, so do we," said a voice at the door. It was Meg, with Janet and Grisie behind her. They crowded into the nursery, looking like girls again in their long nightgowns and wrappers instead of the shimmering silken ball gowns they had worn last night.

"I couldna find Mother at *all*," said Janet indignantly. "She isna in her rooms."

"What was all the commotion?" asked Grisie, yawning. "So early in the morning."

Helen smiled at her. "Aye, I'll warrant ye needed mair rest after dancin' into the night. Yer mither had said I wasna to wake ye this mornin', but to let ye sleep as late as ye liked." She unloaded the tray, setting the dishes neatly upon the table. "O' course, that was before the wickedness happened."

"*What* wickedness?" cried Martha and Meg together. Martha felt like the boggart in the fairy story, who got so upset one day he took hold of his two feet and pulled his own self in half. She couldn't bear not knowing for one more minute.

"Someone," said Helen, and her voice dropped low, "*someone*, and there's no kenning who—though I think Master Harry has his ideas—came in the middle o' the night, after the dance, when all the house was sleeping like the dead, and *uprooted all the master's trees.*"

"What?" Meg gasped. Martha stared openmouthed.

Helen nodded solemnly. "It's true, sure as I breathe. The scoundrels, whoever they be, crept in and pulled up every blessed one o' those trees and flung 'em into a ditch to die. It canna have been the work o' one man. I've nae doubt the laird'll find out who did it, sooner or later, and bring 'em before the judge. But the trees are done for; there's no savin' 'em, I fear."

"But why should anyone do such a thing?" asked Mary, her eyes wide and puzzled.

"Why, indeed," murmured Helen wisely. "Ye'll not be knowin', Miss Mary, how the farmers across the loch fussed and fretted when his lairdship, your uncle, put in the first plantation o' firs, years ago. Sure and I mind hearin' many a foretellin' that the trees would be the ruin o' the land. I heard auld Mr. Hubbard say to me own mither, 'Ye mark my words, missus; that young laird wi' his new-fangled notions will be the end o' Glencaraid. Ev'ry fool alive kens what trees'll do to a piece o' ground. Take over the country all round, they will, and send their roots creepin' into the barley and the oats. We'll all starve to death, lookin' at his lairdship's pretty trees.'"

"But he was wrong," said Martha stubbornly.

"Aye, so he was—and he'd be the first to admit it now. Everyone kens what a blessin' those trees have been to the farm. They break the wind comin' off the mountain, so the soil doesna blow away as it used to. Aye, and the crops are stronger, too. 'Twas only good sense for Master Harry to improve South Loch in the same way."

223

"And someone here thought it a mistake, and took matters into his own hands," muttered Meg in disgust. "It's horrible."

"What's Father going to do?" asked Grisie.

Helen shrugged and pick up her tray. "I canna say. He went down to the village with Master Harry, to question everyone. I'll warrant there are a few knees knockin' out there this mornin'. But I'd best get downstairs before someone comes lookin' for me. We've a great many mouths to feed in this house today. I'll bring yer porridge up straightaway, Miss Janet. Will ye eat here in the nursery, or shall I take it to yer sittin' room as usual?"

"Neither," said Janet sleepily. "I'm going back to bed."

All the rest of that long morning, Martha and the others had to stay cooped up in the nursery. They could hear the noise of the various party guests wandering downstairs to see what kind of breakfast had been laid out in the dining room. Mary and Rachel tried to guess who each person was by the sound of their passing, but Martha felt too distracted to play. She couldn't bear not knowing what was happening down in the village. Father and Uncle Harry had taken their guns. She wished all the more that Miss Crow had come to Fairlie. Miss Crow would know whether or not a gun fired in the village could be heard away up here in the house. Miss Crow was very good at knowing things.

Miss Caldwell came back after a while. She made the girls get out their sewing, and as they stitched she read to them for a very long time from a book of sermons. Her voice was dull and toneless, and Martha did not understand a word of the sermon, except one part that talked about dreadful things happening to naughty, disobedient children. She was rather interested to know exactly what sort of dreadful things were meant, but the author did not seem to have gone into details. After that she got so absorbed in thinking up dreadful things on her own—falling into the fire and burning to a crisp; being carried off by a kelpie to be drowned in its cold and lonely loch; falling beneath a millstone and having your bones ground to powder—that she was quite surprised to realize that Miss Caldwell had closed her book.

"There's been so much excitement this morning, I really think you girls ought to have a nice rest until dinnertime," said Miss Caldwell. "You may lie down, if you wish, or you may continue sewing until I call you. Be nice and quiet, my dears."

Then she left, closing the door behind her.

Martha sighed. Another impossible nap she was expected to take! Excitement, Miss Caldwell had said. But all the excitement was on the other side of that door. Martha wished she were one of the village children, so that she could be down there right now seeing for herself what was happening.

Then it occurred to her that if she were a village child, her own father might have been one of the men who ruined Uncle Harry's trees.

That would be more dreadful than any of the dreadful things she had imagined during Miss Caldwell's sermon.

The Men Who
Killed the Trees

Some of the guests went home, and some stayed to see if anything was going to happen because of the trees, and some stayed because they had come to Fairlie planning to stay for a while. Fairlie was the sort of house that people were always coming to visit. It was lovely and large, and Aunt Grisell's cook was very good. Uncle Harry liked to have guests. He was a jolly man and he liked to have jolly people around him.

But he was not jolly when he came back to the house at last, just after dinner had been set on the long dining-room table. Father came behind him, and his eyes were dark. They entered the dining room from the terrace, bowed to the guests, and said they would just go wash up.

"Dinna wait," said Uncle Harry. "Go on and eat."

Martha and the cousins sat at the low end of the table, trying to be quiet as mice so that no one would send them back up to the nursery. Miss Caldwell sat opposite them and kept up a continual stream of eyebrow liftings and discreet gestures that were intended, as best Martha could tell, to instruct the girls in nice manners. When Miss Caldwell tapped on her closed lips with one finger, that meant "Don't chew with your mouth open." When she held up her napkin and waggled it just the slightest bit, that meant someone had a bit of food on her mouth that needed dabbing off.

The only trouble was that Martha and Mary and Rachel could never tell which of them Miss

Caldwell was signaling, so they had to all three wipe their mouths at the same time. And the sight of three small girls raising their napkins in perfect unison seemed to be irresistably amusing to some of the guests, particularly one red-haired young man with laughing eyes and a very fine waistcoat. Martha recognized him as one of Grisie's dancing partners from the night before. He had a roguish grin that reminded her of her brother Robbie. She knew that he was the son of a laird who lived to the north, near Loch Tay. He seemed to spend very little time eating and a great deal of time smiling at Grisie.

He caught Martha watching him and winked at her. Martha stared back at him with her stoniest glare. She felt outraged by his cheek—making sheep's eyes at Grisie and then winking at Martha as if they were friends.

The young man seemed not to notice he was being glared at.

"Excellent trout, isna it?" he asked Martha amiably.

"I like it better the way our cook makes

it," she heard herself say. Miss Caldwell's mouth fell open in her surprise, revealing a mouthful of fish. Martha nearly choked trying to suppress an urge to tap her lips with a finger.

She was glad Uncle Harry's table was so long. Mum was a great distance away at the other end of the table, absorbed in conversation with Aunt Grisell, the Bigginses, and a distinguished minister from Perth.

When Father returned, Uncle Harry not far behind him, the room fell silent. Even the grinning young man from Loch Tay grew sober and turned his attention to the head of the table. In a grim voice, Uncle Harry told about his visit to the village. He and Father had spoken to every tenant on the South Loch farm. No one had admitted to the crime, of course.

"But we've a fair notion who it was. Allan made every man look him squarely in the eye. There's not many can tell a bald-faced lie to a man's face wi'oot giving himself away wi' a twitch or a blink."

"I ken well enough who it was," said Father. His voice was low and dangerous. "Guilt in their eyes and sap on their hands, they had."

Uncle Harry shook his head wearily. "I ought to have seen it coming. They're the same men who've gone about grumbling ever since I came to Fairlie. Hankering after the auld days, they are, when their only master lived on the other side o' the loch."

"That's just plain foolishness," snapped Mum. "You're Allan's own brother-in-law."

"Aye, and I'm a city man who's never farmed in me life," said Uncle Harry mildly. "It's *that* they canna forgive me for."

"It's not their place to forgive. South Loch is my land, and I can entrust it to the care of whomever I see fit," said Father. He sighed deeply. "Well, we'll see this matter settled soon enough. It's my hope the men who did it will come to me freely and confess. Two o' them have families, and I dinna fancy havin' to send some child's father to prison."

Martha looked at her plate and tried to swallow. She wondered which of the South

Loch men Father was talking about. She knew them all by name; she had played with their children at weddings and festivals. Suppose—

She did not dare to suppose. It was too awful to think that it might be the fathers of some of her own friends who had done this cruel thing to Uncle Harry's trees. She felt grateful that it could not be Ian Cameron's father, nor Lew Tucker's, nor Una Shaw's. Their fathers were not South Loch farmers; they were tradesmen.

"And what will you do if they confess?" demanded Mr. Biggins. "Let them off with a beg-your-pardon-sir?"

"Of course not," said Father curtly. "They'll have to work off every penny o' the cost o' those trees."

Mr. Biggins snorted. "You're too soft on your people, Glencaraid. And this is what comes of it, if you ask me. *Your* father wouldn't hesitate to have these men imprisoned, would he, young MacDougal?"

The red-haired young man took a long sip from his mug before answering. His face was solemn, and the merry light was gone from his eyes.

"*My* father," he said, "has just evicted a dozen families whose people have worked his land for two hundred years and more. Threatened to burn their cottages over their heads, he did, if they took too long about clearing out. He's turning the land over to sheep. There's a great deal more coin in that, you ken, than in having tenant farmers."

The young man's voice was very cold. Mr. Biggins pursed his lips and cleared his throat a little.

"*My* father," the young man continued quietly, "would likely have these men publicly flogged and driven off his land. If you're asking whether I approve o' such methods, I can tell you this: I'd rather be son to the laird o' Glencaraid than to MacDougal o' Tay."

For a long time no one said anything. Martha felt queer and shivery inside. She had never heard of someone wishing his father were not his father. She could not stop staring at the young man.

Perhaps the children of the men who'd killed the trees would wish their fathers were someone else, too. It made her want to run and hug her own father, and climb into his lap like she had used to when she was younger.

She thought of all the times she'd wished her father was a weaver or a farmer instead of a laird. That made the shivery feeling turn to flip-flops in her stomach. *It's not the same thing,* she told herself fiercely. She had never wanted Father to be anyone other than Father. She had only wanted him to have a different station in life, so that she need not be a proper young lady all the time.

But she could not eat any more dinner, not even when Helen brought out a plum pudding for dessert.

Handsel Monday

Grisie and Mum and Martha went home to Glencaraid that afternoon. Father stayed behind at Fairlie. Martha felt very sorry to say good-bye to him. He bent and touched her cheek with one hand, and he told her not to fret over the trees.

"I'll soon set everything to rights, lassie," he said. "We'll plant new trees next year."

Mr. Shaw was waiting with his boat. The wind keened softly over the loch as they crossed, and the droplets of water that splashed off the ferryman's oars were icy cold. Autumn had begun to creep away while Martha wasn't looking.

Soon winter would come and wrap itself around the Stone House. The long, dark months were coming, when Mum's spinning wheel never stopped humming and the peats blazed in the big stone fireplace in Mum and Father's cozy room. Mum would sing songs and tell stories, and Grisie would make a flower garden bloom inside the ring of her embroidery hoop, and Cook would send up trays of roasted apples and nuts. Perhaps Miss Crow would have stories of her own to tell—Martha rather thought she would. Certainly she would read poetry, and she had promised to read to Martha from her big book of Shakespeare's plays. Miss Crow had brought very few clothes with her to the Stone House, but she had brought a good many books. She had set them up upon a shelf in the nursery. Martha pictured the governess sitting in the cozy nursery, her hands cradling a book as tenderly as if it were a new baby, and Martha felt suddenly very glad to be going home.

The destruction of the fir trees was the talk of the Glencaraid farm for a month. Sandy was often sent to the village on errands, and Cook demanded he keep her abreast of the South Loch news. He reported that two of the culprits did, in fact, come to Father and confess, and Father told them that as they had destroyed property that belonged to Uncle Harry, it was to Uncle Harry they would have to make amends. Harry set them to building a stone wall around the rye field to keep the cattle out next spring—a cold, lonely job in the winter when other men were spending long hours beside the fire, smoking their pipes and outdoing each other with wild tales.

A third man, who was widely believed to be the instigator of the tree murders, as Cook had taken to calling it, disappeared without notice not long after the incident. He was rumored to have gone to Perth to board a ship bound for Canada.

"He'll see trees enough over there," snorted Cook, when she heard. "They say that land is one solid mass o' forest for hundreds upon hundreds o' miles. And full o' bears and panthers and wolves, like as not. Eh! You'd not see me set sail for a wild place like that for all the gold in the royal treasury!"

"Miss Crow's brother has been to Canada," said Martha. "He told her all about it in a letter. He's been to a lot of places in America, too: Boston and Tennessee and Kentucky."

"Mercy, they have some outlandish names over there," Cook exclaimed. "But what can you expect from Americans?"

Miss Crow let Martha read all her brother's old letters. They were a glimpse into a magical world, as strange and wild as the fairy kingdoms that were hidden under green hills in all of Cook's stories. Stranger, even, for fairies seemed almost commonplace next to marvelous tales of the Indians who lived in tents instead of houses, and wore feathers and beaded necklaces and animals skins instead of linen. Andrew Crow was a trapper, a fur trader, and his letters were full of stories about the vast American woods. When Martha read them, she wanted to go—she wanted Father to sell his land and take them all across the sea to the New World, where Robbie could be a trapper and Duncan could be a painter and Alisdair could be president like the famous General George Washington.

Then she would catch herself and know that she was once more wishing Father were different, and the jumbly feeling she had felt at Fairlie would come back to her.

One day a rider carried two letters to the Stone House: one from Miss Crow's brother—the first one she had received since she came to the glen—and one from Martha's brothers at school. Andrew Crow wrote that he was in Louisiana, living among the Acadians. He was trapping beaver and fox, and eating spiced crawfish and boiled peanuts. Alisdair wrote that he was earning good marks in Latin and history, and he had decided he'd like to study law if Father would allow it. Robbie wrote a short note that told nothing and asked a great many questions about the estate—how many deer had been killed so far this winter, and how was the hay holding out, and had the spotted dog's puppies grown up all right? Duncan sent a sketch of his schoolmaster, a forceful-looking man whose face somehow managed to appear plump and pinched at the same time. Like all of Duncan's drawings, it managed to say a great deal about its subject in a very few strokes. It certainly conveyed more than his accompanying letter, which said only that he was in good health, his coat was too short in the sleeves, and he had burned his hand with candle wax but it didn't hurt anymore.

Mum shook her head over those letters and laughed and cried all at once.

"Och, the dear lads," she said. "Gracious, how I wish Perth weren't so far away. I must ready a package for Hogmanay. As soon as Cameron weaves up the red wool, I intend to make a new suit o' clothes for each one o' them."

Martha wondered if Gerry, Nannie's husband, would be the one to do the weaving of that wool for his father. Cook said Gerry was such a hard worker that his father had been able to double his business. One of these days, Cook declared, Nannie would be able to afford her own maid. Martha liked to think of that. It was funny to picture Nannie, so merry and humble, giving instructions to a servant. Martha thought she would rather like that job herself, helping Nannie cook the meals and clean the rooms in the cozy little house that Martha had not yet seen.

Hogmanay came—Old Year's Day, the last day of the year—and Aunt Grisell gave another party. The red-haired MacDougal lad was there again, and he danced two reels and a minuet with Grisie. Another young man, who was a bit older than MacDougal and who wore a wig so heavily powdered that he always had a fine sifting of white dust upon his shoulders, hovered at Grisie's elbow and stood glowering in the corner whenever she danced with MacDougal. Martha glared back at him, and she glared at MacDougal, too. She did not like to see these bold young men vying for her sister's attention. But the MacDougal lad only winked at her, and Powdered Wig took no notice of her at all.

The day after Hogmanay, New Year's Day, was Martha's ninth birthday, and after that came Handsel Monday. That was a very special day, for tradition demanded that on that one day, the family had to make breakfast for the servants. This year Mum said Martha and Grisie must do it all themselves.

"You're auld enough now," she said, "and Martha for one certainly spends enough time in the kitchen to ken her way around."

Miss Crow woke Martha very early that morning and pushed her out of bed with a playful shove.

"Mind your apron strings near the fire," she said. "And dinna forget I like my porridge none too sweet."

"Are you not coming down to help us?" cried Martha, incredulous.

Miss Crow laughed and rolled over, fluffing up her pillow.

"I'm one of the household help, Martha," she pointed out. "You have to serve me, too, this morning."

Martha scrambled into her frock and tied on her apron. The room was dark and bitterly cold. Her fingers were stiff, and her breath puffed out in clouds. Most mornings Martha awoke to the sounds of Mollie building up the fire in the nursery hearth. She had never realized what a frosty house Mollie must wake up to each morning.

She ran to Grisie's room and shook her sister awake. Grisie grumbled and burrowed under her covers, but Martha yanked the heavy quilts away and poked at Grisie until she was wide awake.

"Leave off!" Grisie snapped, shivering in her long woolen nightgown. "It's too cold to move."

"It'll be warmer in the kitchen when we get the fire going," said Martha eagerly. "Come, hurry and get dressed! I want to be the one to put on the new peats."

"Go right ahead," shuddered Grisie. "Get yourself all dirty, you will."

The stairs were so dark Martha wished they had brought a candle. But down in the kitchen, a faint gray light was creeping through the eastern windows. The sun was just beginning to come up over the loch.

Grisie lit candles while Martha hurried to the hearth. She dug the banked peats out from under the ashes and poked them with the long iron poker. She always thought of Lew Tucker when she saw that poker, for his father had made it. She stabbed at the smoldering peats to make the sparks fly, just the way she had seen Cook and Mollie do it, and she carried a new square of the dried, matted grass to the hearth and placed it carefully atop the old ones. Soon tiny wee flames began to lick at the edges of the peat, and then they grew bigger and bolder. Grisie and Martha stood close to the fire, rubbing their hands.

They spoke in whispers, for they did not want to wake Cook. Cook's bed was at the far end of the kitchen in a little alcove under the stairs. They could hear her snoring.

"Now what?" asked Grisie in dismay. She looked helplessly around at the array of kettles and knives and meal barrels.

"Porridge," said Martha decidedly. "And

eggs. I saw Cook put some fish in to soak last night; we can flour them and fry them in the big pan."

Grisie blinked at Martha, a little smile playing on her lips.

"Mother's right; you do ken your way around, dinna you?"

Martha felt very happy. She did not care that her feet were frozen and her ears burned with cold. She broke through a skin of ice on the water in the water bucket—the bucket was full to the top, and Martha guessed that Cook had done that on purpose last night to save her or Grisie a trip to the spring—and dipped several dipperfuls of water into the middle-sized kettle that hung from the iron crane in the hearth.

"Let's see," she murmured, counting on her fingers. "There's Cook, Mollie, and Miss Crow—three. Do you think Sandy will come? That's four. And I suppose we ought to make enough for Mum and Father, too."

"I doubt they'll want to eat what we serve," laughed Grisie. "They'll wait for Cook to make a second breakfast, or else go hungry."

"Nay, ours'll be fine," said Martha confidently. "We'll make enough for eight, so we can eat, too. I think we need another peat on that fire, Grisie. This water is never going to boil."

Last year and all the years before, Mum had done most of the cooking on Handsel Monday. Martha had expected that this year Grisie would take charge. She was so very grown-up these days; she acted just like Mum in nearly every way.

But Grisie seemed quite content to let Martha run the goings-on in the kitchen. She kept asking Martha's advice about the simplest little things, until Martha stared amazed at her older sister and wondered how you could grow all the way to womanhood and not know how to bread a fish nor how much salt to add to oatmeal porridge.

By now the sun was pouring in and setting the room aglow. It must have been an hour later than Cook had ever slept in her life, but still the astonishing noise of her snoring came thundering out from the little alcove beneath the stairs. Martha quite forgot to whisper, and she called out commands to Grisie as authoritatively as Cook had ever addressed her kitchenmaid.

"You've got to *stir* the porridge, Grisie, else it'll scorch! Just stay there beside it and keep stirring. Oh dear, I think we've built our fire too high."

Cook's snores had begun to take on a curiously choked sound from time to time.

Martha went to the larder to look for eggs and remembered that the hens had stopped laying months ago. There could be no scrambled eggs, this morning, after all—and she had so looked forward to cracking the shells. But she found a cask of pickled eggs and thought perhaps those would do nicely instead. And there was a cold venison roast under a cloth on the shelf; she carried it out to Cook's table and found the big wicked-looking carving knife to cut slices with.

"It's bubbling, Martha; I think it's finished," said Grisie anxiously. Martha told her to lift the kettle of porridge off its hook and set it upon the hearthstones where it would keep warm.

But Grisie could not lift it; Martha, in her zeal to make sure everyone had enough to eat, had filled the heavy kettle almost to the top.

"What'll we do?" Martha cried, beginning to panic. She could not bear it if the porridge was burned. There was no fouler tasting stuff in all the world than burned porridge.

Cook's snoring had ceased for a moment, and the girls looked at each other in the quiet.

"I have it," said Martha suddenly. "We need only swing out the crane so it hangs over the floor instead o' the fire. Happen the pot willna keep as warm that way, but . . ."

"Aye, better than scorching it," said Grisie, and she found a thick towel to wrap over the end of the crane so she could swing it around. "Gracious," she said, sighing with relief. "I dinna ken how Cook can do this every day and keep her wits together."

Then she and Martha burst out laughing at the same moment. Martha could almost hear

Cook's harried voice barking out commands to Nannie and grumbling that she'd work herself to death one of these days.

"What's left to do?" asked Grisie. Her long, dark hair was loose about her face, and there was a glop of oatmeal caught on one side. Her cheeks were flushed and rosy, and her eyes sparkled. Martha thought her sister was prettier than she'd ever seen her. She was fiercely glad that neither the MacDougal lad nor old Powdered Wig could see Grisie now.

"Bread the fish and fry it," she answered. "Finish slicing the meat. Sugar the porridge— but not too much. I wish we had bannocks so we could give them some jam. I wonder do we have time to make some?"

"Heavens, nay," said Grisie hastily. "I think we'll have quite enough, with the porridge and the venison and the fish."

"And the pickled eggs," Martha added in satisfaction. "Aye, it's a grand spread. And I ken what we'll do—we'll open a jar of blackberry preserve and let everyone eat it with spoons."

From the alcove now came the queerest sounds of snoring they had ever heard.

"I think she's waking up," whispered Martha, forgetting that she had been talking at the top of her voice a moment before. "Hurry, you go and set the table. I can do the fish."

Grisie hesitated doubtfully, but Martha gave her a shove and she hastened to the parlor. Working as quickly as she could, Martha mixed oatflour and salt and pepper on a plate. She tried to think whether Cook put anything else in to season the fish when she made it, and after a moment's consideration she went to the larder and climbed up on a stool to reach the bundles of dried herbs that hung upside down from the rafters. She broke off a few stalks of thyme and some chives. She was not sure if those were the right seasonings for fish (though she did know, for Auld Mary had taught her, that the thyme would cure gout and earache), but they were the only ones that hung low enough for her to reach. Quickly she ran back to the work table and

250

crumbled a fair amount of each herb into the flour mixture.

She took the fish out of their soaking-water and rolled each one in the breading; and then with great effort she hauled Cook's big frying pan onto a trivet over the fire. In went a dollop of bacon fat from the crock Cook kept against the wall, and while it melted in the pan Martha opened the cask of pickled eggs and scooped a dozen or so into a large white serving dish.

Grisie returned and said the table was laid, and she carried the eggs, the venison, and the jar of preserves into the parlor. Martha's bacon fat was sizzling now, so she hurried over with the plate of breaded fish and scraped them, extra breading and all, into the pan. They hissed in a most satisfying way. They were the first dish she had ever cooked all by herself, the dear little things. She felt positively fond of them.

"Anything else?" asked Grisie. "I think I hear them stirring upstairs."

"And there's Sandy!" cried Martha, for the front door was scraping open in the hall. She looked at her fish and wondered how to tell when they were done and she shouted to Grisie to find a platter to put them on.

"We'll have to dish up the porridge in here," she said with regret. "The kettle's too heavy to carry to the parlor fire. Och, nay! We forgot to start the fire in there!"

They stared at each other in dismay. Grisie looked helplessly at the sizzling fish, and at last she said in a voice of dread, "I'll go and light it. Oh dear, I hope I dinna burn down the house."

"Just stir up the smoldering peats and put a new one on top," said Martha encouragingly. "It's easy."

Grisie sighed. "All right. I suppose we could have Sandy carry the porridge in for us."

But Martha cried, "Nay! We must do everything all ourselves!"

She turned back to her dear fish and saw that the extra bits of breading had made a sort of paste in the bottom of the pan. Grabbing a serving fork, she tried to turn the fish to brown their other sides, but they stuck to the skillet. She had to scrape and push to get the fork beneath each one, and when she turned them the breading came off in large patches. But the rest of the breading was a lovely golden brown, and when Grisie came back from lighting the parlor fire, flushed and soot-smudged, she said the fish looked truly delicious. There was surprise in her voice, so that Martha could see she really meant it.

"Go call Mum," said Martha. "I think we're nearly ready."

And just in the nick of time, for at that moment Cook's snoring gave way to an enormous noise of yawning and stretching. Never in her life had Martha heard such a loud waking up.

Hastily she checked the underside of the fish, burning her finger in the process. The bottoms were not quite as lovely as the tops; they were a dark brown, not golden, and in some places unmistakably black. Martha scooped them onto her platter and tried to arrange them so that the black parts didn't show. She wasn't sure whether to include the flour paste or not, but it smelled rather nice so in the end she scraped up as much of it as she could and shook it off the spatula onto the dish, where it lay in clumps like little golden brown mountains around the fish.

She heard Cook's feet clumping loudly on the floor in the alcove and Cook's voice muttering to herself about how late the hour was. Martha wondered if perhaps Cook had forgotten today was Handsel Monday. She stood grinning in the middle of the floury, grease-spattered, smoky kitchen and waited to see the surprise on Cook's face.

Cook staggered out of her nook, rubbing her eyes and sighing wearily.

"Och, there's nivver a day's rest in this life," she was grumbling, "and me sae tired and weary I can hardly put one foot in front o' t'other. I suppose I'd better get the porridge on—saints preserve us! What's this!"

There was real shock on her face as she took in the scene. Her eyes roamed over the untidy kitchen and came to rest upon Martha, flushed and proud with her platter of fish in her hands.

Cook threw back her head and laughed and laughed.

"Och, ye'd think an army o' children had marched through this place, instead o' just the two," she said. "Is that fish I smell, Martha? Sure and ye've gone to a lot o' trouble for yer auld Cook this bright and airly mornin'!"

"Aye, we made fish and I fried it all myself!" Martha cried out in triumph. "See?"

She held the platter out proudly for Cook to inspect. Cook's mouth twitched uncontrollably.

"Aye, I see," she said, chortling. "Ye dear sweet lamb. I wonder ye didna burn yourself to a crisp."

"Only one burn," said Martha happily. "And I scorched my apron a little. But come and see the rest!"

She ushered Cook into the hall, where they met Mollie and Miss Crow coming down the stairs, Mum and Father close behind them.

Martha noticed for the first time that Cook was wearing her good Sunday dress. So were Mollie and Miss Crow. Grisie was standing in the parlor doorway, beaming in excitement.

"Come and eat, before it gets cold," she said. "Sandy's inside already."

The sight of the parlor table took even Martha by surprise. Grisie had quite outdone herself. She had spread out Mum's best table-cloth, the one with the embroidered border of fruits and berries and birds. At each end she had placed a pair of silver candlesticks in which burned tall, fragrant beeswax candles, and in the middle was a beautiful arrangement of dyed ostrich feathers in a vase. The feathers had been her Hogmanay gift from Father, and he looked pleased as anything to see them so gorgeously displayed.

The dishes of food looked quite plentiful in the midst of that lovely table, and Cook cooed and wiped her eyes, and Miss Crow said she'd never been treated to a finer break-fast feast. No one mentioned how cold the room was—for Grisie's fire, which flickered weakly in the hearth, had not yet managed to take the nighttime chill out of the room. Everyone sat down, with Sandy at the head of the table and Cook at his right hand, in Mum's chair. Father made a joke of taking Martha's seat as if he were the youngest and least important person there. Martha found herself opposite Miss Crow in the middle of the table, and she looked around in delight to see how different the room looked from this seat. She had never taken much notice of the pictures on the far wall before. One of them was an oval portrait of some long-dead MacNab ancestor. For the first time, Martha saw how the jowly old gentleman with the little sausagelike curls by his ears had something of Father in his eyes: a calm, friendly, steady gaze that meant he had everything well in hand. Martha found herself liking that funny old man a great deal and feeling as if she had known him a long time.

Sandy said grace, and the food was passed round. Everyone praised the lopsided slices of venison and the crispy fried fish.

"Mmm, excellent porridge," said Miss Crow. "Quite a nice texture to it, it has."

Grisie laughed remorsefully. "Has lumps, you mean. That's my fault—Martha did keep telling me to stir."

"It'd be all right if it hadn't grown so cold," Martha said, wrinkling her nose.

"Nonsense, it's perfect," growled Cook. She would not allow a single criticism of the meal. She ate two servings of the lumpy porridge and two servings of the fish, flour paste and all.

"What'd ye season this with, Martha? It's no my recipe, but it's aye delicious, it is."

"Chives and thyme," she said happily. She didn't let on that she had chosen those herbs because they were the only ones within her reach.

"Really?" said Cook. "That's a new one! Truly, lass, it's as tasty a morsel o' fish as ivver I've eaten."

Everyone else agreed, and Martha could see that they meant it. When she tasted it herself, she was surprised to find that it really was quite good. She felt glowing inside.

She sat looking up and down the table, watching the others take hearty bites of the fish and the venison and the sweet, rich preserves. It felt like feasting, just watching them eat.

Grisie's Suitors

A good many horses made their way around Loch Caraid that winter; the Stone House had never had so many visitors before. Some of the visitors were guests of Uncle Harry and Aunt Grisell who wanted to spend a little time with Mum and Father. Others were young landowners who came to speak with Father about the new ideas in agriculture. It was well known throughout the county that Father was a man who cared more about his land than his house and that he was making bold experiments with new crops such as the versatile American cotton.

Kenneth MacDougal, the red-haired laird's son, was a frequent visitor, and he spent many an evening in earnest conversation with Father. Martha had a private suspicion that he came as much to see Grisie as to see Father. But it was true that Kenneth was also quite interested in what Father had to say.

He was eager to hear about the new threshing mill Father had seen on his last trip to Perth, and what sort of diet Father kept his cattle on during the winter. His own father, he frankly admitted, had all but given up on farming. The sweeping MacDougal lands had been turned over to sheep, whose wool fetched a fine price from the merchants who traded with the new spinning mills down in Glasgow. Kenneth had vowed that when he inherited his father's estate, he would return the land to the people who had farmed it for centuries. Those people, he said, had been loyal to the MacDougal chief for time out of mind. Now the old clans were disappearing, and the lairds had become businessmen instead of protectors.

"I canna bear it," Kenneth MacDougal said passionately at dinner one day. "It seems the auld Scotland is fading away. The landowners have traded loyalty for a full purse, curse them!"

The fire in his voice made Grisie clasp her hands in sympathy, but Mum said mildly, "You want to go softly, lad. You dinna want to find yourself cursin' your own father. There's more than one kind o' loyalty, ye ken."

"I tell you, Mrs. Morse, sometimes I feel I'm the cursed one. How can I love him as my father and hate him as my laird? What he's done to his people is cruel, and there's nae denying it."

Father nodded soberly. "Aye. It is wrong. But you're duty bound to honor him all the same. You must seek out a way to open his eyes to truth instead o' blinding him with anger."

Kenneth MacDougal was quiet for a long time, looking down at his plate.

"Aye," he said at last. "It's easier said than

done. I'm half blind wi' anger myself, much o' the time."

He shook himself a little, like a dog coming in from the rain. The roguish gleam came back to his eye.

"So, Miss Martha," he said slyly. "How do you pass your days, now the flax season is past?"

He had heard the flax-bundling story some-where—Uncle Harry most likely, or Grisie—and had relentlessly teased Martha about it ever since.

"Miss Crow and I are reading the plays of Shakespeare," she answered, refusing to rise to the bait. "We're doing *King Lear* now. I'm learning bits of it by heart."

"Och, *Lear*, is it? A favorite of mine. Isna it a bit much for a delicate wee lass, though, all that death and tragedy?"

"Nay," said Martha firmly. "I love it. Only I wish that Cordelia had a bit more backbone to her."

"Martha favors the outspoken characters," said Miss Crow, smiling.

263

"There's a surprise," quipped Kenneth. Grisie giggled.

"Well, come then, let's hear a bit," Kenneth added. "You said you're learning it by heart."

Martha searched her mind for a passage. The things her parents had said to Kenneth about his father made her think of a line, and she could not resist saying it.

"How's this?" she asked saucily, and quoted,

> *"How sharper than a serpent's tooth it is*
> *To have a thankless child!"*

Kenneth's eyes went wide.

"Martha!" cried Grisie in horror, and Father roared with laughter.

"That'll teach you to spar wi' my daughter, young MacDougal!" he said. "Martha, you're a terrible impudent lass, and you ought by rights to be locked in a closet for the rest o' the day."

Kenneth's face was as red as his hair. He shook his head, chuckling. Grisie glared at

Martha, but Mum's laugh rippled across the table. Miss Crow seemed very busy with her napkin.

"Mortally wounded by a nine-year-old," Kenneth said, clapping a hand to his heart. "Martha, I pity the young men who must dine at your table when you're nineteen."

"When I'm nineteen," said Martha, "I'm going to go and be a cook somewhere, and make puddings and roasts and pies all day."

"Martha!" This time it was Mum crying out in reproach. Father's laughter died away, and he frowned a little.

"You'll not have to work for your bread, Martha, you ken that. Whatever would put such a thought in your head?"

"Nothing, Father. It wasna a thought. It's only that I like to cook."

She did not understand why everyone looked so grave.

"Wee lasses have a great many notions that fade as they grow," said Miss Crow softly, smiling at Father. "When I was nine, I declared

I would grow up to be a ship's captain. We must all of us grow into the shoes we were born to, mustn't we?"

Kenneth MacDougal raised his glass. "Hear! Hear!"

Martha's toes wriggled inside her black boots. She did not understand in the slightest what Miss Crow was talking about. Her boots had come from Perth; she had not been born to them. Anyone might have seen them in the cobbler's window and brought them home to his little girl, as Father had brought them home to her. They had not been made especially for her. She wished they had; they might fit better, instead of pinching at the toe.

Kenneth MacDougal began to visit more and more often. He had just stabled his horse one day in March when two other gentlemen and a lady came trotting up the hill on beautiful brown stallions. One of the men was the jowly Powdered Wig, whose name turned out to be Archibald Leggett, and the other was a much older man who had identical jowls. He was Powdered Wig's father, and the lady was his mother. Her bonnet had such a wide brim that when she climbed off her horse and stood on the ground, Martha thought she looked like a mushroom with a very long stem.

The visitors arrived just before dinner, sending Cook into a frenzy in the kitchen. She bustled around, fretting about not having enough roast to go round and thanking the Lord that Sandy had brought in such a nice mess of eels that very morning.

Martha kept very quiet at dinner. There was no teasing or jesting with Archibald Leggett. He gazed solemnly at Grisie and made occasional remarks about the many fine hunting dogs he had at home. He steadfastly refused to look at Kenneth MacDougal. Grisie looked mostly at her own plate. Sometimes her eyes glanced up at Kenneth, and Martha saw how her sister wanted to laugh with him about the owlish Archibald Leggett. Archibald's father talked for a long time about the goings-on in Parliament. His mother did not speak at all, except to praise the eel stew.

After dessert Mollie cleared the table and

everyone moved to the soft chairs at the other end of the parlor. A cheerful fire crackled in the hearth. Father poured goblets of claret for the guests, and Archibald implored Grisie to sing for them. Grisie went shyly to the pianoforte. She played and sang, and Kenneth MacDougal applauded loudly, and Archibald glared at him with cold, dull eyes.

Martha grew fidgety upon her seat. Miss Crow came to her rescue and said politely that she and Martha ought to return to the nursery to continue their lessons. Mum nodded, but Kenneth MacDougal cried out, "What? No recitations today?"

"Oh, do you recite?" asked Archibald's mother. "Do let us hear a wee something."

Martha squirmed. She liked to recite, just not in front of people like the scowling Archibald Leggett.

But Mum said, "Go ahead, Martha. Give us 'Tam o' Shanter.'"

So Martha had to go and stand before the fire with everyone's eyes upon her. She took a deep breath and began—

When chapman billies leave the street,
And drouthy neebors neebors meet . . .

The poem's first lines told about nightfall in a village, when the street peddlers called chapmen packed up their wares for the night, and drowsy neighbors chatted with other neighbors, and the village folk began to settle down for the night. Kenneth MacDougal sat listening with a delighted grin on his face, and Father looked very proud. Martha began to enjoy herself. She spoke the words with force and meaning, the way Miss Crow had taught her. After a verse or two, even Archibald Leggett lost his scowl and began to look interested.

Martha told how foolish Tam o' Shanter sat too late in the tavern with his mates, so that it was past midnight by the time he set out through the woods for home. She came to the fearful scene in which Tam's mare, the faithful Maggie, raced through the dark trees with the pack of witches close behind her and Tam hanging on for dear life. Everyone was leaning forward a little in their chairs. Archibald's eyes goggled whitely and his hand made a little slapping motion at his side as if he were spurring on his horse. Martha saw it and it made her like him a little. It meant there was something to him besides the powder and the scowl.

At last Maggie came to a stream. If only she and Tam could get across it they would be saved, for the witches could not cross running water, so the legends said.

> *There, at them thou thy tail may toss,*
> *A running stream they dare na cross!*

But the leading witch came fast behind the poor horse—

> *And flew at Tam wi' furious ettle;*
> *But little wist she Maggie's mettle!*
> *Ae spring brought off her master hale,*
> *But left behind her ain grey tail:*
> *The carlin claught her by the rump,*
> *And left poor Maggie scarce a stump.*

Martha's voice rang with triumph as she spoke those lines. That was her favorite part, when the witch grabbed furiously to pull Tam off the horse's back, unaware of how much courage and strength there was in old Maggie. Maggie sprang over the stream and saved her master—though it cost her her own tail, for the witch caught hold of it at the last second and pulled it right off.

When Martha had finished, Kenneth MacDougal whistled and stomped his feet.

"I declare! You've made the gooseflesh come out on my arms," he said admiringly.

After that Martha and Miss Crow went up to the nursery, and Miss Crow taught Martha how to put gathers in a skirt. Martha had come to enjoy sewing lessons, for while they stitched, Miss Crow told stories about the olden days in Scotland, when the great clan chiefs had waged fierce battles against each other, and people had had to live inside walled fortresses to keep safe from attack. An afternoon spent that way could pass in the blink of an eye, and Martha was surprised to realize that the sun was sinking low and still the guests lingered in the parlor.

"Are they staying the *whole* night?" she asked Miss Crow. She could not think why they would not rather stay at Fairlie, where there was an abundance of beds.

"I expect it's the two young men," said Miss Crow wisely. "Neither one of them wants to be the first to leave."

"But that's silly," protested Martha.

Miss Crow nodded. "You'd best prepare yourself for an onslaught of silliness, Martha, for there's naught sillier than a young man in love."

"In *love*?" Martha screeched.

"Hush, lass! Would you have them hear you down below?"

With an effort Martha lowered her voice to a whisper.

"Are they in love with Grisie? *Both* of them?"

"'Twould be my guess. I'm surprised you hadn't surmised as much. Mind your needle,

Martha, it's about to fall to the floor."

Martha sat for a while poking little holes into the cloth.

"Is she going to get married?" she whispered at last.

Miss Crow looked her in the eye. "I expect so, Martha. Sooner or later. You must have realized that before now."

"I kenned she would someday. Only I thought we'd be grown-up first."

"Grisie *is* grown-up, my dear." Miss Crow's voice was very gentle. "Or nearly so."

Martha frowned.

"I hope she has the sense to pick Kenneth, then," she said furiously. "I couldna bear having that old Powdered Wig for a brother."

The Lads Come Home

Gug-gug, said the cuckoo,
On Beltane's yellow day.

That was the first of May, when all the girls in Glencaraid went out at dawn to wash their faces in the dew. Cook baked bannocks that morning marked with crosses on one side. Martha and the cottagers' children assembled on the grass at the top of the Stone House hill and took turns rolling their bannocks down the slope. Martha held her breath as she watched her bannock careen

274

over the steep grass, for it was very bad luck for your bannock to break on the way down. Fortunately Cook's bannocks were baked with the wisdom of many a Beltane Day behind them; she had left them longer than usual in the frying pan, so that they were tough and sturdy. These bannocks, after all, were not meant for eating.

Only one boy—Annie Davis's cousin Bert— went home with a glum face and the heavy weight of impending bad fortune upon him, his bannock having struck a rock and shattered into a hundred fragments. The little brown sparrows flocked to the hillside for their own Beltane feast.

Martha listened all day for the cuckoo, but she didn't hear it for another day or two, when its cheerful song came sailing over the garden wall while she and Miss Crow sat mending stockings under the plum trees. Miss Crow exclaimed in delight, for she had lived in the city for many years and had heard no cuckoos since she was a small girl herself.

"The merry cuckoo, messenger of spring,
His trumpet shrill hath thrice already
sounded,"

she quoted. "Listen, there he calls again. He's trying to catch up to the sonnet."

Indeed, the cuckoo called out a third time, and then they saw him fluttering away. Martha and Miss Crow burst out laughing.

"I suppose he feels he's done his day's work," said Miss Crow. "Spring has been announced. And a glorious spring it is. Just look at those trees!"

The plum trees in the Stone House garden were a mass of ruffled white blossoms. The garden smelled wet and green, and there was a rich, wet earthen smell, too, for Sandy had been busy turning over the soil in the vegetable beds. Miss Crow and Martha brought their sewing out to the bench against the plum wall every afternoon now, and Martha was amazed at how swiftly the hours flew by, in spite of the stitching. Miss Crow had set her to making an embroidery sampler, to display all the new stitches she had learned that winter. While the birds chirped and chattered in the lacy white branches above, a proud and stately peacock appeared bit by bit on the creamy white linen in Martha's embroidery frame, his dazzling blue-and-green tail spread like a fan.

Day after day the glen grew greener, and the tiny yellow buttercups peeked out of the grass. The wooded slope of Ben Fallon was carpeted with bluebells beneath the slender white birches, so that the wood was like a royal hall arrayed in splendor for a fairy queen. Miss Crow took Martha up to the slope one day and read to her from one of Shakespeare's plays, a story about another fairy queen and her king, and the strange things that happened to the mortals who wandered into their woods. Grisie had been coaxed along, too, and after a bit she set aside her handwork and sat listening with her fingers clasped in her lap like a little girl.

The ninth of June was St. Columba's Day,

The day to put sheep to pasture,
To warp the loom, and to put cow to
calf.

The sheep were indeed driven out to the green slopes on the shoulders of the mountains, with the eager black-and-white sheepdogs circling joyfully behind them and the shepherds shouting and waving their crooks. Many of the Glencaraid cottagers began packing for their move to sheiling, the summer cow pasture in the high mountain glens. The great, shaggy, long-haired cattle stamped their feet and bellowed in the barnyard, as if they, too, were impatient to return to the high meadows. Martha stayed outside every minute Miss Crow would allow her to, and often Miss Crow would go out with Martha to watch the cattle, and the sheep, and the farmers' plows making dark brown stripes of earth in the fields.

And finally it was summer, and the school

holidays came at last. Father and Sandy went
to Perth on their twice-yearly trip for supplies,
and they came back with a cartload of sacks
and packages, and Martha's brothers besides.
Martha hardly recognized Alisdair and Robbie.
Robbie had grown so tall and thin that at first
glance she thought he was Alisdair with his
hair turned dark. But then she realized that
the even taller stranger being hugged half to
death by Mum was Alisdair, and her heart lol-
loped in shock.

"Alisdair!" she cried out. "You're all grown!"

Alisdair laughed. His neck was long and
skinny, and his voice cracked when he spoke.

"Not quite all grown. I'm still not so tall as
Father."

"Saints preserve us, these lads are naught
but skin and bones," Cook clucked. She had
abandoned a roasting hare in the kitchen and
pushed in among the family to claim her own
round of hugs. "Dinna they feed ye in that
cursed school?"

She cast an accusing glare at Father, which
set him laughing.

"You've a month to fatten them back up, Cook," he said teasingly.

"That I shall do, and ye can be as certain o' that as sunup and sundown," Cook said severely. "Startin' this very night."

Even Duncan was taller. Except for that, he looked the same as he always had. Martha asked him if he had made any pictures of Perth to show her, and his eyes lit up.

"Aye, near a dozen o' em! I've got a ship under full sail in the harbor—it's me best drawing yet. You ought to see the great huge ships, Martha; big as whales, they are!"

When Mollie had unpacked the boys' trunk, Duncan spread out all his paintings for Martha to see. She felt swelled up with pride for her brother: the drawings were so lifelike. His paintings were better than Miss Crow's brother's letters. She felt, too, a wild and sweeping longing to go to Perth and see for herself the buildings and streets and ships he had painted. Glencaraid was the bonniest, dearest valley in all Scotland; but there were wonders and marvels out there in the wide world beyond the mountains and the moor. She wanted to see them with her own eyes, so that the picture of them would be painted in her mind forever.

She told Duncan and Robbie all about Grisie's suitors. They scoffed at the thought of young men hanging about, hoping for a smile or a soft word from their older sister.

"Imagine our Grisie an old married lady!" Robbie demanded.

"I dinna like to imagine it," said Martha. "She'll go away and live somewhere else, like you, and then I'll be all alone."

The next day Mum made all three boys put on their red Hogmanay suit jackets, so that she could see for herself how they fit. Martha hooted with laughter, for all her brothers lacked were powdered wigs to make them as fine and fancy as the young men who came to Aunt Grisell's parties. Duncan escaped in disgust to the kitchen as soon as he could, to see if he could coax a cake or two out of Cook.

Then he and Martha went down to the loch together. They saw a boat coming across the loch; it was Lewis and Ian, come to see Duncan. They cheered and halloed from the boat, waving their caps in the air, but when they arrived on shore a strange awkwardness arose between the three boys. Martha stood a little way off, puzzling over how stiffly they greeted each other, how hesitantly they spoke.

Ian stood shifting from foot to foot, taking in Duncan's fine trousers and his bright new coat. Ian's own father had woven the woolen cloth for that coat; probably Ian himself had helped to put the warp on the loom. A look Martha could not read came into Ian's eyes; his hand had gone up to punch Duncan on the arm in the friendly way they had always greeted each other, but it froze before it touched the red jacket.

Duncan and Lew wore the exact same shy, embarrassed looks upon their faces. Martha saw that there was something between them all which had never been there before. She did not know what it was. She only knew that the boys did not shout and wrestle as they had used to do. She supposed all of them were thinking about that fine new coat.

Ian's shuffling and Lew's quiet eyes were suddenly too much for her to bear, and she burst in among them, calling out in a voice that was too loud.

"Now Duncan's home, we can have Picts and Scots on the Creag again. We've not played that in ever so long—not since you went away, Duncan! And there've been no footraces either, have there?"

She was surprised to suddenly realize that. In springs past the village boys had always come over to her side of the loch for games and races with Martha and Duncan and the cottagers' children. But this year they had not come once.

"You're afraid I'll beat you yet, Lew Tucker—I'll bet that's why you've stayed away," she said boldly. She only said it because she did not know what else to say. She hated the strangeness that hung between them all. Hadn't they all been friends their whole lives?

Her challenging words had brought out a slow, quiet smile upon Lew's face.

"Ye say so, do ye?" he said softly, grinning. "Think I'm a coward, is that it?"

His blue eyes laughed; he was enjoying the joke.

"Nay!" Martha protested. "I didna say that!" Of course she did not think Lew Tucker was a coward. He was one of the most stouthearted lads in the valley; everyone said so.

"I'm no certain ye did not," Lew teased. "But I'll forgive ye your harsh words, Miss Martha, that's all right."

Ian and Duncan were laughing, too, now.

"Go on, race her," jeered Ian. "Else we'll think ye are scared, Tucker. Happen ye've grown soft, living easy in the forge all winter."

That was a joke between Lew and Ian; Ian liked to tease Lew that Mr. Tucker's blacksmithing work was a stroll in the meadow compared to the arduous task of weaving. Of course he did not really mean it, for anyone with one eye open could see that a blacksmith's job was anything but easy. The scorching heat of the forge, the tireless swinging of the heavy hammers—a smith, it was said, must be stronger than the iron he worked.

"How bold you are, Martha," laughed Duncan. "I thought your governess was meant to teach you some manners."

"The first one couldna; the second'll likely have no better luck," said Ian. Martha laughed right along; she did not mind being teased, for it meant that horrible awkwardness had gone away.

"Miss Crow ought to teach *you* some manners, Ian Cameron," she retorted. "She ought to teach the lot o' you. When a *lady* makes an invitation, the proper thing to do is to accept."

"A lady!" hooted Duncan and Ian together.

But Lew grinned again and said, "All right, then, Miss Martha. I accept your kind invitation. Let's have us a race. Shall we start on t'other side o' the Creag, where the ground's level?"

"Aye," said Martha firmly, wondering if there was the slightest possibility that she could, in fact, run faster than Lew. He was three years older and a good deal taller than she was. And he was the fastest runner in the valley.

But she strode toward the Creag with her head held high. She'd not let it be said by anyone that she was afraid of a challenge—particularly not when she herself had been the one to issue it. As they passed the Glencaraid cottages, Annie and Finlay and some of the other children came running to join them, so that by the time they reached the open moor beyond the Creag a small mob had formed to watch the race. Everyone knew that Martha had boasted she could beat Lew Tucker, and all the children were eager to see if the laird's little daughter could truly outrun the blacksmith's strong son.

Duncan drew a line in the turf with his boot to mark the starting point, and Ian jogged a good distance away to mark the finish. He stood on the line with his arms outstretched; the first to pass him would be the winner.

The other children spread out along the course to watch, cheering and shouting.

"Go on then, Miss Martha, teach him to

mind his place!" cried Annie, leaping into the air in her excitement.

"She'll nivver do it," called one of the boys. "Her legs are too short."

"That only makes her lighter," Duncan said haughtily, forgetting that he had been on Lew's side in the beginning. Of course, he could not root against his own sister, not when there were others around.

"Will I give ye a head start?" asked Lew politely. "It's only fair, seein' as I'm sae much older."

Martha tossed her head indignantly. "I should think not! And dinna you go slower just to be nice, either. I shan't need your help to beat you, Lew Tucker."

Lew's good-natured grin shone at her again. "All right, then. Let it be as ye say."

Martha tucked up her skirts beneath the sash of her apron. Her heart was pounding as if she'd already been running. She had not meant for every child in Glencaraid to watch this race.

Duncan stood at the starting line, looking

grand as a laird in his fine crimson coat. He raised his arm in the air, and all the children grew quiet.

"Take your marks—ready—go!"

Martha ran. She ran as fast as ever she could run. Lew was ahead of her, but she tried not to think of his strong legs carrying him away. She made herself into a deer, skimming over the ground. Ian seemed a great distance away. He was as small as a brownie, jumping up and down and shouting. She could not hear what he was saying; she couldn't hear anything, only the pounding of her heart.

Lew was too far ahead; she would lose, and lose badly. Somehow she made herself run faster, and the gap between them closed a little. Pain was wrenching at her side, and her skirts were slipping out from the apron sash. Her hair ribbon had come out, and her hair streamed behind her like a horse's mane.

She thought of Tam o' Shanter on his mare. She was the horse, Maggie, running wild-eyed with the witches behind her. That thought was so terrible that she found she could run

faster after all. No witch would catch *her*, no foul, evil, sulfurous witch.

Lew was not very far ahead now.

"Yaaaaa! Martha!" Annie was screaming. Martha could hear again suddenly, and there was Ian very close by. She was nearly there. She was beside Lew; she would pass him, she would—

He slapped Ian's hand just ahead of her. Lew had won.

Martha slowed to a halt, panting, her hair flying wild in her face. Damp tendrils clung to her neck, and her lungs were screaming. But she did not mind. Lew had beaten her, but only by a little.

He turned toward her with a broad, glad smile that was all for her and didn't have anything to do with his own victory.

"Ye near had me," he said admiringly. "I dinna think there's a lad in the village who's come sae close."

"Not even I," said Ian. "That was a grand show—and ye such a wee thing."

The children came crowding around them

to cheer and clap them on their backs. Duncan brought her the lost hair ribbon and said she'd done the Morses proud.

"Only dinna expect Grisie to think so," he added, laughing. "Most likely she'll faint dead away when she hears what rough games her sister's been up to. Her suitors mightn't like it."

"Pah!" scoffed Martha. "Then they've no business courting her, if they're as fussy as all that. "

The Cottage
Beyond the Wood

Summer was in full bloom when Martha's brothers returned to Perth, for their school holidays were short. The slope beneath the Stone House was bright with thistle and heather, blue cornflower and golden yarrow. Martha and Miss Crow sat in the flowery grass, well away from any thistles, watching the little fishing boats dance upon the waters of the loch. Martha taught the governess a song about yarrow flowers she had learned from Auld Mary:

> *I will pluck the yarrow fair,*
> *That more benign shall be my face,*
> *That more warm shall be my lips,*
> *That more chaste shall be my speech,*
> *Be my speech the beams of the sun,*
> *Be my lips the juice of the strawberry.*

"By all means we must pluck some," Miss Crow told Martha. "How lovely to think of one's words shining like sunbeams!"

"Yarrow looks like sunbeams," said Martha. "So nice and warm and yellow."

"And these cornflowers are like little bits of sky," said Miss Crow. "What's the name of the little pink blossom there? Beside the big stone."

Martha told her it was called mouse-ear.

"Auld Mary used it in a poultice on Gavin Tervish's leg yesterday," she said. "He brought his hatchet down in the wrong place and made a terrible wide gash. But Auld Mary says it'll mend."

"I know. Auld Mary came to the kitchen this afternoon," said Miss Crow, "while you were upstairs with your mother. She thought perhaps you and I could deliver a parcel for her on the morrow. She doesn't wish to leave Mr. Tervish for long until the fear of infection is past, but her parcel cannot wait. No one else has quite the leisure you do, and she thought you might enjoy the walk, besides."

"Aye, I would!" cried Martha gladly. "Where are we to go? We shall go, shallna we?"

"If your mother gives us leave," laughed Miss Crow. "It's a syrup of coltsfoot for Mrs. Gow in the north glen. Her husband sent word that she's got a bit of a cough, and she's scarcely three weeks out of childbed, the poor woman."

"I ken just where she lives," said Martha. "Och, Mum *must* say we may go."

Mum did say so. She came down to the kitchen and filled a large basket with presents for the sick woman: a large wedge of cheese, a jar of jam, some raisins, a loaf of bread, a small crock of fresh butter, and Auld Mary's cough syrup. Martha wanted to carry the basket but it was too heavy. Cook clucked her tongue and bustled into the larder, and she came back with a smaller basket covered over with a napkin.

"Cakes for the wee ones," she said. "Dinna ye eat them all on the way there, Martha."

"I'd never!" said Martha indignantly.

Cook shrugged placidly. "Sure and I did put in enough for ye to have one or two," she added. "Ye'll need something to stay yer stomach on the long walk."

Miss Crow did not know the way to the northern tip of the valley. She had never yet been past the hay meadow. Martha led her across the burn and alongside it, north along the edge of the wide flax field. The flax had bloomed once more into a broad ribbon of sky. It seemed a very long time ago that Martha had worked alongside the cottagers, bundling the stalks. She wondered where Miss Norrie was now, and whether she had found a good little child to care for.

"Will you stay here always?" she asked Miss Crow.

Miss Crow smiled, but she did not say anything just at first. They walked in silence for a few moments, the baskets quietly rocking on their arms.

"It's not likely I shall," said Miss Crow at last, in her frank way. "You'll not need me forever, Martha. And I've a notion to go to America to see my brother, someday."

Martha blinked hard, scowling. She could not speak.

"But," said Miss Crow, "I shall stay here a good long while. Your parents and the good Lord willing, of course. We shall have years together yet, Martha. So I'll not stand for any fretting now, mind. And"—she looked side-ways at Martha, her gray eyes twinkling—"if ever you learn to write a letter without smear-ing, then you shall write to me wherever I go, and wild horses could not prevent my answer-ing you."

Martha could not help but laugh. She still hated copywork. It took such a long time to write neatly, and even when you were writing out beautiful passages from Shakespeare or the Bible, you were still merely repeating the lovely thoughts that had come from someone else's mind, not your own.

She thought perhaps she would like writing letters better than copywork. She could tell Miss Crow everything that was happening in Glencaraid—who was ill, who was getting married, how many acres Father was giving over to cotton, how Uncle Harry's new fir trees were coming along. The possibilities were so appealing that she had almost packed Miss Crow's trunk and sent her across the ocean before she thought what she was doing. It would be nice to write Miss Crow someday. She did not want that day to come anytime soon.

Beyond the flax field was another wide field, this one planted with turnips and potatoes. Annie and some of the other tenant children were weeding between the rows. Martha waved at them but did not stop to talk. Everyone was very busy.

She was glad to be busy herself, on such an important errand. Her steps quickened, for she thought of poor Mrs. Gow coughing in her lonely hut, with the new bairn and her other small children to care for while her husband was away in the fields, earning their bread.

The tilled land gave way to a sparse hilly wood, and the valley grew narrower. The steep slopes of the mountains rose craggy and green on either side. Martha and Miss Crow kept close to the bank of the burn, where the moss grew thickly on the gray stones and the arms of the rowan and elder trees reached overhead. Harebells grew in thick clusters between the trees. Their flowers, like little blue hats just the right size for a fairy, bobbed in the breeze. Mum said the wee flower bells chimed a warning to hares when danger was near. When she was very little, Martha had often crouched beside harebells with her ear nearly to the ground, listening for that faint tinkling, but she had never heard anything. She supposed it was a magic chiming that only rabbits could hear.

The Cottage Beyond the Wood

After another mile or so, the stream dipped suddenly around the curve of a hill, and just on the other side was the Gows' cottage. It was a thatched house made of mud and turf, just like the houses of the tenants who lived by the loch. This house, however, was not so neat and trim as Mrs. Sandy's hut or the Tervishes'. Martha had heard from the cottagers that Mr. Gow was a bit of a sluggard. It was clear that he had neglected to take proper care of his house. The hut's thatch was shaggy and thinning, and there were gaps between the layers of turf in the walls. A skinny dog lay in the open doorway, worrying a bit of leather with his yellow teeth. Beside him squatted a small, sooty child wearing a shirt that must have belonged to his father, for it hung down below his knees and trailed in the dirt. The sound of a baby frantically screaming rang out from inside the cottage.

"Good heavens," said Miss Crow. The little boy looked up, and his eyes widened at the sight of Martha and the governess.

"Our minnie's sick," he said. "Sorcha says she's dyin'."

"Your mother is dying?" gasped Martha.

"Let us hope Sorcha is wrong, whoever she may be," said Miss Crow firmly, hastening toward the hut. She squeezed past the dog, who paid her no mind except to lift his tail lazily and thump it once upon the ground.

The boy was still staring at Martha. His eyes went to her basket, and he said in a hopeful tone, "Is there anythin' to eat in there?"

"Cakes," said Martha, reaching into the basket. "Here, take one. Our cook made them; she's the best cook in the county; everyone says so."

She gave him one of the soft, currant-studded cakes and watched him devour it in a very few bites. She was glad she had not eaten any of the cakes herself. The truth was she had not remembered them, for the walk had been so pleasant and her belly was contentedly full from the good breakfast of porridge and cream and eggs Cook had sent upstairs. She wondered when was the last time this little boy had tasted fresh cream. Martha had pools of it on her porridge every day, as much as she wanted.

"There's cheese and things in the other basket," she told the boy. "I ought to go see if I can help."

The baby was still crying, and Miss Crow's confident voice murmured out from the cottage.

"Can I have another cake?" asked the boy. "I wish me minnie could eat 'em; I bet they'd make her well in a minute. Sorcha tried to give her some broth, but she coughed so much it all came back oot."

Martha gave him another cake and went slowly into the house. Her eyes squinted to see in the dim light. There was a strong, sour smell inside, and the air was very close. The floor near the doorway was muddy where rain had blown in, and the fire was out.

"Martha, here, take the bairn," Miss Crow commanded. "I wish we'd brought some milk. It's ravenous, the poor thing."

Shocked, Martha clutched at the tiny

screaming bundle that had been thrust in her arms. The red-faced baby was wrapped in a bit of coarse linen. Its little fists waved in the air. Martha tried to rock it, crooning one of Mum's songs softly under her breath. The baby turned its head toward her and opened its swollen angry eyes a slit. She sang a bit louder, but it would not stop crying. It only subsided to a pitiful whimper that was a kind of giving-up sound. There was a lump in Martha's throat, but she dared not stop singing.

She had been too absorbed with the baby at first to notice anything else inside the cottage. But now she saw that it looked very much like Mrs. Sandy's hut, except that Mrs. Sandy's home was a great deal tidier. There was one large room divided by a turf wall that went only partway up from the floor, leaving a large space between the top of the wall and the ceiling. The smaller chamber was meant for the family's cows, Martha knew, but it was empty now, and it looked as if it had been empty for a long time.

The Cottage Beyond the Wood

The fireplace was a simple ring of stones in the middle of the larger room. A few plain wooden benches were drawn up near the hearthstones, and an iron pot hung from a chain over the place where the fire should be. But the ashes were cold; there was no fire.

Against one wall were several straw mattresses. Upon one of these lay a woman. Her hair was matted and damp, and her eyes were frightened. Her breath came in hoarse gasps, and every few seconds her body was wracked with a terrible grating cough. Miss Crow knelt beside her, tucking a blanket over her. A little girl about five years old crouched by the woman's head, her small, lean hand stroking and stroking her mother's hair.

"You'll be all right now, dear," Miss Crow was saying. "We've brought you one of Auld Mary's nice tonics to take away that nasty cough. And we've got bread and cheese and such a nice bit of butter in the basket, for you and your wee ones. Where is your husband, my dear?"

Mrs. Gow tried to answer but another wave

303

of coughing swept over her, and her body bent nearly double on the coarse mattress. The little girl picked up a mug of water from the floor beside her and held it anxiously in both hands, waiting for her mother's coughs to subside.

Cradling the baby carefully, Martha went to kneel beside the little girl.

"Are you Sorcha?" she asked.

The girl nodded. Her eyes were very large, and her face was as solemn as an owl's.

"Our minnie canna talk for coughin'," she said. "Me da's been gone to Crieff these two days past. She was nivver so sick when he left us."

Mrs. Gow nodded weakly and murmured something in a pale, whispery voice. Miss Crow had to bend close to hear her.

"Don't fret, dear. We'll look after the little ones. Do you think you can swallow a bit of this syrup?"

She asked Sorcha for a spoon, and the girl pointed to a shelf on the far wall. She would not budge from her mother's side. Miss Crow went to look for the spoon and then she rummaged through Mum's basket for the bottle of coltsfoot syrup.

The little boy had come inside the hut, standing silently in the doorway, watching. When Miss Crow went back to Mrs. Gow's pallet, he crept up to the big basket and peered inside. Martha saw him, but she could not put down the baby.

"Sorcha," she said softly, while Miss Crow poured a spoonful of syrup, "there's a loaf o' bread wrapped in that red napkin, and butter in the little crock. Do you think you could cut yourself a slice, and one for your brother?"

Sorcha nodded, and her eyes stared hungrily at the basket, but she would not leave her mother. The little boy grabbed the basket by its handle and, small as he was, dragged it over to his sister. He went to the table and brought back a knife. Martha watched with her heart in her throat for fear he would trip over his father's long shirt, but he carried it safely to Sorcha. She unwrapped the bread and, spreading the napkin on the dirt floor beside her, set the loaf upon it and cut three thick, uneven slices. Eagerly she smeared butter on each slice and gave one to her brother.

"Can ye eat a bit, Minnie?" she asked plaintively, but Mrs. Gow shook her head and coughed and coughed.

"I'll make some broth," said Miss Crow decisively. "You got the syrup down, that's a mercy. It'll soon soothe the coughing, you'll see, and then perhaps you can nurse Baby."

Tears streamed from Mrs. Gow's eyes. "Thank—," she tried to say, but the terrible coughing overtook her again.

Miss Crow gestured for Martha to follow her to the door. The baby had at last ceased its crying and was dozing fitfully in Martha's careful arms.

"She's a good deal more ill than we knew," whispered Miss Crow in Martha's ear. "Auld Mary must come and see her, for I fear she needs something stronger than coltsfoot syrup. Mr. Gow ought not to have left her like this when she was just taking ill. He's gone to see some traveling players in Crieff, I gather, or some such foolishness." Her breath huffed out angrily. "But there, I suppose he couldn't have known it would get this bad. It's a mercy he stopped at Mrs. Sandy's and asked her to have Auld Mary send the tonic. "

"Will she be all right?" Martha asked desperately. She felt a terrible lump inside her chest. They ought to have come yesterday. She remembered sitting outside, enjoying the pretty weather, and all the while Mrs. Gow was lying here coughing herself to death with no one to care for her children. "Can Auld Mary cure her?"

"I dinna ken, Martha. I pray that she can." Miss Crow reached a tender hand toward her to stroke the baby's flushed face.

"Here's what we must do," she continued. "We need Auld Mary, and a lot of other things besides. Mrs. Gow must have a good strong beef broth to put some strength back into her, and the children ought to have milk and eggs and kale. And a good thick blanket from your mother's chests, for the one on the bed is thin as paper. Clean linens for the bairn. A sack of meal wouldn't hurt; I'll warrant they havena got much here.

"I can see to things here, Martha—I dare not leave Mrs. Gow. But you'll have to go back for Auld Mary and the supplies. Can you do it alone? The quicker the better."

"Of course I can!" Martha flashed. "I'll run all the way."

Miss Crow nodded confidently. "Just mind you don't make yourself ill, lass. I thank the Lord you're not a fearful child."

Miss Crow told Martha to wait until she got a fire going, and then she would take the baby. Martha watched the children eating the last crumbs of their slices of bread and licking the butter off their fingers. Sorcha took up the cup of water again and held it lovingly to her mother's lips. Mrs. Gow managed a few swallows, and she smiled weakly at her small daughter.

Martha thought about Annie and Mrs. Sandy and all her friends in the cottages by the loch. Martha supposed that when Mrs. Gow wasn't sick she kept her hut as neat and tidy as Mrs. Sandy did. She could see it in the anguished way her eyes looked out at the disheveled room. It was strange to think how suddenly things could go wrong, when you did not have friends close around you. If Mrs. Sandy took sick, all the other cottagers would know about it in a minute, and Auld Mary would come right away. If Mum took sick, there would be a whole house of family and servants and friends to nurse her. Cook would work her fingers to the bone to make Mum nourishing things to eat, and Mollie would sit up all night to keep the fire burning bright. And Mum would never have to worry that her children would go hungry while she lay ill.

As soon as the fire was crackling and Miss Crow had put on a kettle of water to boil, Martha handed over the baby. She said good-bye to Mrs. Gow and the children, but she doubted anyone could hear her above the coughing. Then she took off running.

She ran around the green hill and back through the woods, past the harebells and the mossy stones of the burn. Her lungs burned inside her, worse than they had the day she raced Lew Tucker. She did not need to pretend she was Tam o' Shanter's mare today. That terrible cough in the cottage behind her, and the hungry wails of the bairn—those things were worse than any pack of fairy-tale witches.

The Mare's Ride

The front door of the Stone House stood open, and Martha clattered inside without slowing down. She had expected to find Mum upstairs in her room, but as she passed the parlor doorway she heard music and glimpsed a crowd of people around the pianoforte. Grisie was playing.

Martha burst into the parlor and clutched Mum's arm, panting furiously. A sharp stitch tore at her side with each breath. The music stopped suddenly and a ring of faces turned to look at her in irritated surprise. Father's eyes were angry, and Mum looked shocked.

"Martha!" she cried out. "What in heaven's name—"

Martha gasped for breath. She couldn't yet speak. She bent forward, hands on her legs, trying to catch her breath, and her hair tumbled wild and tangled over her shoulders. She had tucked up her skirt and her petticoat so as to run better, and she could feel everyone looking at her bare legs.

Mum and Father had guests again: the ever-present Kenneth MacDougal, and a lady and gentleman Martha did not know. All of them were staring at her in varying degrees of horror. Grisie's face was flushed with misery and embarrassment. Only Kenneth MacDougal did not look dismayed; he was grinning his broad, impertinent grin.

"*Martha!*" roared Father. "Have ye no manners whatsoever? What on earth are ye playin' at, lass?"

At last Martha found her voice. "It's Mrs. Gow," she gasped. "I've just come from her place. She's terribly ill, Mum, near dying!"

Mum's hands flew to her mouth. "What? Surely you've not had time to get there and back already?"

"Aye, I did. I ran all the way home."

"From the Gow place?" Father whistled. "That's more than three miles, lass."

"Aye," Martha said again, panting. It was all she could say.

"That's well run," murmured Kenneth MacDougal.

"What's this about Mrs. Gow?" Mum asked, coming forward to smooth the hair out of Martha's face and to straighten her bunched-up skirts.

"Miss Crow says we must have milk and a blanket and eggs and beef. And I must go find Auld Mary straightaway," Martha said urgently. "Do you think she's still with Mr. Tervish? Mrs. Gow is far worse than we imagined, Mummy; she can hardly breathe for coughing, and the bairn is starving, and the wee ones are so brave but I ken they're frightened for their minnie."

It had all poured out in a tumble, but Mum

seemed to take it in stride.

"Grisie, send Mollie to the Tervish place to fetch Auld Mary. I'll go set Cook to packing another basket. Beef, you say? Aye, and we'll send a mutton roast as well. Allan—?"

She looked at Father, and Father seemed to know just what Mum was thinking, for he nodded sharply and said, "Aye, I'll take Auld Mary there myself."

"On your horse?" Martha cried, a wave of hope and joy rushing over her heart. Now Auld Mary would be sure to get there in time to help the dying woman.

But when Mollie came hurrying back from the Tervish cottage a few minutes later, she said Auld Mary had returned to her hut for an ointment to put on Gavin's wounded leg.

"Blast," muttered Father. "I'll have to go there first."

"I'm worried about that bairn," said Mum. "I ought to go myself and see if I can help."

Kenneth MacDougal slapped his hands together. "I tell you what, Lady Glencaraid—

I'll take you there on my horse, and the laird can go fetch your herb-woman. I beg your pardon, Grisie; you'll forgive my running off like this."

"I certainly will," said Grisie fervently, her eyes gleaming. Martha took in the look that passed between her sister and the young man, and his tender "Grisie" echoed in her mind. Since when had Kenneth MacDougal begun to call Grisie by her first name?

But she did not have time to think about it. Kenneth's plan was readily assented to, and Mum made hasty apologies to her guests. The strange lady and gentleman turned out to be Kenneth's parents—Martha could hardly take it in. This handsome, silver-haired old man looking down at her so amiably was the cold-hearted laird who had set his people's houses afire over their very heads?

She wondered if *he* would be so quick to saddle his horse to help a poor sick tenant. She felt grateful for her own father's kind heart. She was glad it was Father who was laird of Glencaraid, and not the MacDougal. Mrs. Gow would likely die, if Kenneth's father were her laird.

Mum hurried upstairs to slip into a gown more suitable for riding than her delicate, buttercup-yellow silk. Father bid his guests good-bye and said, "Come along, Martha. You're coming wi' me in case Auld Mary needs to send for anything else from your mother's stores."

Martha could hardly believe it. In her whole life she had only been given a handful of rides on Father's beautiful horse—and then nothing more than sedate walks around the yard. This ride would be different. And to be taken along on such an important errand—it meant she was needed. Father needed her.

Sandy had been informed of all the goings-on, and he brought Father's horse, saddled and ready, to the yard in front of the house. Martha stared at the mare, feeling caught up between so many different emotions that she was afraid she would burst into tears like a bairn. It was such a lovely surprise, being taken for a ride on the black mare. But to be happy at such good fortune, when it' had only come about because a woman was in danger of death, with no one to care for her newborn babe—a pang of guilt stabbed at Martha's heart. Was it wicked, she wondered, to be glad of *anything* at such a time?

Father came out of the house. He looked at Martha, and his eyes were tender.

"Dinna fret, lass. 'Twill all come right, ye'll see. We'll get Auld Mary there in time, and your mother is already on her way. Between them, they'll set things right, I've nae fear. Come then, we'd best be on our way."

Martha nodded. She knew Father wouldn't say such a thing if he did not believe it to be true. She felt calmer. Mrs. Gow would be all right.

Father lifted Martha onto the black mare's glossy back, and then he swung up behind her. The mare tossed her head and nickered. Martha felt the strong muscles rippling under her hands, and for a moment she forgot everything but riding the horse. She felt dizzy with the joy and excitement of it. From so high up, the world looked different all around. It was like standing on top of the Creag, only better, because this mountain moved and breathed and, when Father had given the reins a mighty shake, ran like the very wind.

All her life she had wanted to soar like the birds that wheeled above the glen. Now she was soaring. She was flying—flying not *away* from something, like Tam on his mare nor even like Mum's mother racing for her life and her children's lives with enemy soldiers on their trail—but rather flying *toward* something, toward prayers that she, Martha of Glencaraid, could help to answer. Father's arms were strong on either side of her. She felt her hair streaming out against him. She felt the wind pulling at her body, the cool rushing air, like the arms of the sky. She had never loved anything so much as she loved this: riding before Father on the great black horse.

The knot that had been in her stomach since she saw how sick Mrs. Gow really was began to unclench itself. Auld Mary would know just what herbs and roots to brew into a medicine that would soothe that horrible wracking cough. Mrs. Gow would be all right; Father had said so. Sorcha and her little brothers would not lose their minnie.

Martha wondered what Mr. Gow would think, when he came home. She wondered what Father would say to him. She did not think she would like to be in Mr. Gow's shoes.

She had never been more glad that her father was her father. She would not like to be Sorcha Gow, with a father who would not take care of the thatch on his own roof, any more than she would like to be the child of one of the men who had killed Uncle Harry's trees. She thought of Kenneth MacDougal, who loved his father but could not be proud of him.

Martha was very proud of her father. No other man in Glencaraid could come to Mrs. Gow's aid the way her father could. He was the laird; and moreover he was the sort of laird who would leave important guests at a moment's notice to rush to help a poor tenant.

She clutched at his arm and squeezed tight, not because she was afraid of falling off the horse, but because she was so glad he was her father.

The mare raced past the cottages, where the women came to their doorways to watch the laird go galloping by. Martha saw Annie, home from the turnip field for dinner, waving and calling her name. Annie's brothers called out enviously. Quick as they flashed past, Martha could see their longing for a ride like hers. There wasn't a child in Glencaraid who would not trade places with her in an instant.

That was something people had been telling her all her life, but she had never understood it before.

It seemed hardly three heartbeats before they had passed the Creag and come out onto the moor at the very spot where she had raced Lew Tucker. She remembered how she had tried to make herself into a horse that day. It had been wonderful, but it had been nothing like this. The beautiful sleek mare, her glossy head leaning into the wind, and the wind sweeping Martha's worries away just as it had swept away the rainclouds on the morning of Nannie's wedding—no, there was nothing like this in all the world.